It was n................ound. The
heat incr.............. seemed to be beyond human
endurance. It was as though a mighty furnace had burst
and set the earth on fire. Ginger turned away. His face
felt raw, his nostrils smarted, his skin itched, and his eyes
were dry and sore.

'We're being buried,' he told Biggles in a choking
voice. 'The sand is piling up on the car.'

'I was afraid of it,' said Biggles, who had tied a
handkerchief over the lower part of his face. 'The car is
filling with sand, too.'

'Is there nothing we can do about it?'

'Nothing. It's just one of those things.'

Captain W. E. Johns was born in Hertfordshire in
1893. He flew with the Royal Flying Corps in the
First World War and made a daring escape from a
German prison camp in 1918. Between the wars he
edited *Flying* and *Popular Flying* and became a writer
for the Ministry of Defence. The first Biggles story,
Biggles the Camels are Coming was published in 1932,
and W. E. Johns went on to write a staggering
102 Biggles titles before his death in 1968.

www.kidsatrandomhouse.co.uk

BIGGLES BOOKS
PUBLISHED IN THIS EDITION

BIGGLES DEFENDS the DESERT

CAPTAIN W.E. JOHNS

RED FOX

Red Fox would like to express their grateful thanks
for help given in the preparation of these editions to Jennifer Schofield,
author of *By Jove, Biggles*, Linda Shaughnessy of A. P. Watt Ltd
and especially to the late John Trendler.

BIGGLES DEFENDS THE DESERT
A RED FOX BOOK 0 09 993840 5

First published in Great Britain as *Biggles Sweeps the Desert*
by Hodder and Stoughton 1942

This Red Fox edition published 2003

1 3 5 7 9 10 8 6 4 2

Copyright © W E Johns (Publications) Ltd, 1942

Red Fox Books are published by Random House Children's Books,
61–63 Uxbridge Road, London W5 5SA,
a division of The Random House Group Ltd,
in Australia by Random House Australia (Pty) Ltd,
20 Alfred Street, Milsons Point, Sydney, NSW 2061, Australia,
in New Zealand by Random House New Zealand Ltd,
18 Poland Road, Glenfield, Auckland 10, New Zealand,
and in South Africa by Random House (Pty) Ltd,
Endulini, 5A Jubilee Road, Parktown 2193, South Africa

THE RANDOM HOUSE GROUP Limited Reg. No. 954009

A CIP catalogue record for this book is available from the British Library.

Printed and bound in Great Britain by
Cox & Wyman Ltd, Reading, Berkshire

Contents

Contents

To the
CADETS OF THE AIR TRAINING
CORPS

many of whom will soon be carrying on
the Biggles tradition, as those already
in the Service carried it during the
Battle of Britain, and are still 'Venturing
Adventure' above the near and
distant corners of the earth.

The word 'Hun' used in this book was the generic term for anything belonging to the German enemy. It was used in a familiar sense, rather than derogatory. Witness the fact that in the R.F.C. a hun was also a pupil at a flying training school.

W.E.J

Chapter 1
A Desert Rendezvous

So slowly as to be almost imperceptible the stars began to fade. The flickering rays of another day swept up from the eastern horizon and shed a mysterious twilight over the desert that rolled away on all sides as far as the eye could see. Silence reigned, the tense expectant hush that precedes the dawn, as if all living things were waiting, watching, holding their breath.

Suddenly a beam of light, tinged with crimson, began to paint the sky with pink, and simultaneously, as though it were a signal, from the north-east came the deep, vibrant drone of aircraft. Six specks appeared, growing swiftly larger, and soon resolved themselves into Spitfires* flying in Vee formation.

From the cockpit of the leading machine Squadron-Leader Bigglesworth, better known in the R.A.F. as Biggles, surveyed the wilderness that lay beneath, a desolate, barren expanse of pebbly clay and sand, sometimes flat, sometimes rippling, dotted with camel-thorn bushes, and sometimes broken by long rolling dunes that cast curious blue-grey shadows.

The rim of the sun, glowing like molten metal, showed above the horizon. With it came the dawn-wind, and almost at once the aircraft began to rise and fall, slowly, like ships riding an invisible swell. The sky

* Legendary single-seat RAF fighter from World War Two armed with guns or a cannon.

turned to the colour of polished steel, and the desert to streaming gold, yet still the planes roared on. Once Biggles toyed with the flap of his radio transmitter, but remembering his own order for wireless silence, allowed it to fall back. Instead, he glanced at his reflector to make sure that the machines behind him were still in place.

The rocking of the planes became more noticeable as the sun climbed up and began its weary toil across the heavens, driving its glittering lances into a waterless chaos of rock and sand, sand and rock, and still more sand. But Biggles was looking at the watch on his instrument panel now more often, and the frown of concentration that lined his forehead dissolved as an oasis came into view, a little island of palms, as lonely as an atoll in a tropic sea. His hand moved to the throttle, and as the defiant roar of the aircraft dropped to a deep-throated growl, its sleek nose tilted downwards. Soon the six machines were circling low over the nodding palms, from which now appeared half a dozen men in khaki shirts and shorts, and wide-brimmed sun helmets.

Biggles landed first, and taxied swiftly towards them. The others followed in turn, and in a short while had joined the leading machine, which had trundled on into a narrow aisle that had been cleared between the trees.

Biggles jumped down swiftly, stretched his cramped limbs, and spoke to a flight-sergeant who, having saluted, stood waiting; and an observer would have noted from their manner that each enjoyed the confidence of the other, a confidence that springs from years of association—and, incidentally, one that is peculiar to the commissioned and non-commissioned ranks of British military forces. Amounting to comradeship and

10

sympathetic understanding, the original backbone of discipline was in no way relaxed, a paradoxical state of affairs that has ever been a source of wonder to other European nations. The N.C.O.* was, in fact, Flight-Sergeant Smythe, who had been Biggles' fitter on more than one desperate enterprise in civil as well as military aviation.

'Is everything all right, flight-sergeant?' inquired Biggles.

'Yes, sir.'

'Did the stores arrive as arranged?'

'Yes, sir. Flight Lieutenant Mackail brought most of the stuff over in the Whitley**. He has flown the machine back to Karga. He told me to say that everything is okay there, and he will be on hand if you want him.'

Biggles nodded. 'Good. Get the machines under cover. Fit dust sheets over the engines and spread the camouflage nets. Send some fellows out to smooth our wheel tracks with palm fronds. I hope they understand that no one is to set foot outside the oasis without orders?'

'Yes, sir. I've told them about the risks of getting lost in the dunes.'

'That's right; moreover, we don't want footprints left about. Is there some coffee going?'

'Yes, sir. I've put up the officers' mess*** tent near the spring. It's a little farther on, in the middle of the palms.'

'Did you bring that boy of yours with you?'

---

* Non-Commissioned Officer eg a Sergeant or a Corporal.
** A long range night bomber with a crew of five.
*** The place where the officers meet for eating and relaxing together.

11

'Yes, he's here, sir. He's got the radio fixed up, and someone is always on duty, day and night, listening.'

'What about petrol?'

'It's all here, sir, in the usual four-gallon cans. I didn't dump it all in one place. I had half a dozen pits dug, in different parts of the oasis—in case of accidents.'

'Good work, flight-sergeant. I'll have another word with you later.'

As the flight-sergeant moved off Biggles turned to the five officers who were standing by. 'Let's go and get some breakfast,' he suggested. 'I'll tell you what this is all about.'

In the mess tent, over coffee and a cigarette, he considered his pilots reflectively. There was Flight-Lieutenant Algy Lacey, Flight-Lieutenant Lord Bertie Lissie, and Flying-Officers Ginger Hebblethwaite, Tug Carrington, and Tex O'Hara, all of whom had fought under him during the Battle of Britain.

'All right, you fellows,' he said at last. 'Let's get down to business. No doubt you are all wondering why the dickens we have come to a sun-baked, out-of-the-way spot like this, and I congratulate you on your restraint for not asking questions while we were on our way. My orders were definite. I was not allowed to tell anyone our destination until we were installed at Salima Oasis, which, for your information, is the name of this particular clump of long-necked cabbages that in this part of the world pass for trees. Even now, all I can tell you about our position is that it is somewhere near the junction of the Sudan, Libya, and French Equatorial Africa*.' Biggles broke off to sip his coffee.

* Now Chad.

12

'As most of you know,' he continued, 'a fair amount of traffic, both British and American, is passing from the West Coast of Africa to the Middle East. Most of it is airborne, and it is that with which we are concerned. This oasis happens to lie practically on the air route between the West Coast and Egypt. Over this route is being flown urgent stores, dispatches, important Government officials travelling between home and the eastern battlefields, and occasionally senior officers. It is quicker than the sea route, and—until lately—a lot safer. The route is about two thousand miles long, and the machines that fly it are fitted with long-range tanks to make the run in one hop. We are sitting about midway between the western and eastern termini—which means that we are a thousand miles from either end. For a time, after the route was established, everything went smoothly, but lately a number of machines have unaccountably failed to arrive at their destinations. They disappeared somewhere on the route. No one knows what became of them.' Biggles lit a fresh cigarette.

'Our job,' he resumed, 'is to find out what happened to them, and that doesn't just mean looking for them—or what remains of them. There is a mystery about it. Had one machine, or even two, disappeared, we might reasonably suppose that the pilot lost his way, or was forced down by structural failure or weather conditions; but during the past month no fewer than seven machines have failed to get through, and the Higher Command—rightly, I think—cannot accept the view that these disappearances are to be accounted for by normal flying risks. They believe—and I agree with them—that the machines were intercepted by hostile aircraft. After all, there would be nothing remarkable in that. It would be optimistic to suppose that an important air route like this could operate indefinitely without word of it reaching the ears of the enemy. Naturally, they would do their utmost to prevent the machines from getting through. There is no proof that such a thing is happening, but it is a possibility—I might say probability.'

Here Algy interposed. 'Suppose enemy machines are cutting in on the route; surely it's a long trip down to here from the enemy-occupied aerodromes in North Africa?'

'You've put your finger on something there,' agreed Biggles. 'My personal opinion is that the Nazis, or Italians*, have detailed a squadron or a special unit to take up its position near the route in order to patrol it and destroy any Allied machine it meets. You will now realise why we are here. The machines that fly over this route must go through, and our job is to see that they go through. If an enemy squadron is operating down here, then we must find it and wipe it out of the sky. They will get an unpleasant surprise when they discover that someone else is playing their own game. At the moment we hold the important element of surprise. Assuming that enemy aircraft are operating in this district, they do not know we are here, and I am anxious that they should not know. That's why I forbade the use of radio on the way. Ears are listening everywhere, even in the desert. One message intercepted by the enemy might be enough to give our game away, and even enable him to locate us. Well, that

---

* From 1940 to 1943 the Italians, under the fascist dictator Mussolini, formed an alliance with Hitler and joined in the battle against Britain and her allies.

briefly is the general line-up, but there are a few points that I must raise.' Biggles paused to pour himself another cup of coffee.

'We are out here in the blue absolutely on our own, to do as we like, a free-lance unit. The rest of the squadron is at Karga Oasis, nearer to the Nile. I sent them there to be in reserve, as well as to form a connecting link with the Air Officer Commanding Middle East. I thought six of us here should be enough. Spare machines, stores and replacements are at Karga; they include a Whitley, converted into a freight carrier, for transport purposes. There is also a Defiant*. I thought a two-seater might be useful on occasion, and the Air Ministry very kindly allowed me to make my own arrangements. Angus Mackail is in charge at Karga. He has with him Taffy Hughes, Ferocity Ferris and Harcourt. Flight-Sergeant Smythe is here, as you saw, with a section of good mechanics to look after us. That son of his, young Corporal Roy Smythe, who did so well with us up in the Baltic**, is in charge of the radio, which, however, will be used only for receiving signals.'

Biggles finished his coffee.

'The first thing I want to impress upon you all is this,' he continued. 'We are in the desert—never forget that. To get lost is to perish miserably from thirst. The sun is your worst enemy, as it is the enemy of every living creature in the desert. The sun dries your body. While you can drink you can make up for the loss of moisture, but the moment you are denied water thirst

---

* British two-seater fighter carrying a rear gunner in a four-gun turret. It had no forward-firing guns.
** See *Biggles in the Baltic*.

has you by the throat. Twenty-four hours at the outside—less in the open sand—is as long as you could hope to survive without a drink, and death from thirst is not an ending one would choose. Every machine will therefore carry a special desert-box, with food, water, and anti-thirst tablets, in case of a forced landing. No one will move without a water-bottle. That's an order. If you break that order, any of you, you won't have to answer to me; as sure as fate the sun will turn on you and shrivel you up like an autumn leaf. Don't ever say that I haven't warned you. And, believe it or not, it is the easiest thing in the world to get lost. On the ground, you could get hopelessly lost within a mile of the oasis. As far as possible we shall operate in pairs, so that one can watch the other; but there will, of course, be times when we shan't be able to do that. There's another reason why I don't want people to wander about outside the oasis. Footprints and wheel tracks show up in the sand, and we don't want to advertise our presence to the enemy. If they discover us we shall soon know about it; we shall have callers, but instead of leaving visiting cards they'll leave bombs. Everyone will wear a sun helmet. Keep in the shade as far as possible. Expose yourself, and the sun will blister the skin off you; the glare will sear your eyeballs and the heat will get on your nerves till you think you're going crazy. Apart from the sun, we have another enemy in the *haboob*, or sandstorm. Algy and Ginger have been in the desert before, and they know what it means, but the rest of you are new to it—that's why I'm going to some trouble right away to make sure that you understand what you are up against. That's all for the moment, unless anyone has any questions to ask?'

'Can I ask one, old warrior?' put in Bertie.

'Certainly.'

'Assuming that the jolly old Boche* is polluting the atmosphere along our route, is there any reason why he should choose this particular area—if you see what I mean?'

'Yes. If he operated at either end of the line his machines would probably be seen. It seemed to me that he would be likely to aim for somewhere near the middle, because not only is the country uninhabited, but it happens to be the nearest point to German-controlled North Africa—at any rate to Libya, where there is a German army.'

'Yes—of course—absolutely,' muttered Bertie. 'Silly ass question, what?'

'Not at all,' answered Biggles. 'Well, that's all for the moment. We'll have a rest, but everyone will remain on the alert ready to take off at a moment's notice. I've arranged for a code message to be radioed when the next transport machine leaves the West Coast for Egypt, or vice versa. Naturally, machines operate both ways over the route. Until we get such a signal we will confine our efforts to reconnaissance, noting the landmarks—such as they are. There is at least one good one. The caravan route, the old slave trail, as old as the desert itself, passes fairly close, running due north and south. All the same, the only safe plan in desert country is to fly by compass. Reconnaissance may reveal some of the lost aircraft, or the remains of them.'

'Say, chief, what about Arabs?' inquired Tex. 'Are we likely to meet any, and, if so, what are they like?'

'To tell the truth, I'm not sure about that,' Biggles

* Slang: derogatory term for the Germans.

admitted. 'There are wandering bands of Toureg—those are the boys who wear blue veils over their faces—all over the desert. They are tough if they don't like you. Our best policy is to leave them alone in the hope that they'll leave us alone—hark! What's that?'

There was a brief attentive silence as everyone jumped up and stood in a listening attitude. But the matter was not long in doubt. An aircraft was approaching.

'Keep under cover, everybody,' snapped Biggles, and running to the door of the tent, without going out, looked up. For a full minute he stood there, while the roar of the aircraft, after rising in crescendo, began to fade away. There was a curious expression on his face as he turned back to the others, who were watching him expectantly.

'Now we know better how we stand,' he said quietly. 'That was a Messerschmitt 109*. He was only cruising, so I imagine he was on patrol. It would be waste of time trying to overtake him—no doubt we'll meet him another day. I don't think he spotted anything to arouse his suspicions or he would have altered course—perhaps come low and circled. I'm glad he came along, because the incident demonstrates how careful we must be. Had anyone been standing outside the fringe of palms he would have been spotted.'

'But sooner or later we shall be seen on patrol,' Ginger pointed out.

'That may be so,' agreed Biggles, 'but to be seen in the air won't provide a clue to our base. This is not the only oasis in the desert. Well, that's all. We'll

---

* German plane often abbreviated to ME. The main German single-seat fighter of World War Two.

have a look round the district when we've fixed up our quarters.'

Chapter 2
Desert Patrol

Over early morning tea the following day Biggles planned the first operation.

'No signal has come in, so as far as we know at the moment we have no aircraft flying over the route,' he remarked. 'That gives us a chance to have a look round. I don't expect enemy opposition; if there is any it will be accidental, and for that reason we needn't operate in force. It would be better, I think, if we started off by making a thorough reconnaissance of the entire district, or as much of it as lies within the effective range of our machines—say, a couple of hundred miles east and west along the actual route, and the district north and south. Keep a sharp look out for wheel tracks, or any other signs of the missing machines. Algy, take Carrington with you and do the eastern section. Fly on a parallel course a few miles apart; that will enable you to cover more ground; only use radio in case of really desperate emergency. Bertie, you make a survey of the northern sector. Don't go looking for trouble. There are one or two oases about up there, but you'd better keep away from them—we don't want to be seen if it can be avoided; information travels fast, even in the sands. Tex, you fly south, but don't go too far. I don't think you'll see much except sand. Everyone had better fly high—you can see an immense distance in this clear air. I'll take Ginger and do the western run. All being well we'll meet here again in two hours and compare notes. That's all, unless anyone has any questions?'

No questions were asked, so in a few minutes the engines were started and the six machines taxied out to the open desert for the take-off. Algy and Tug Carrington took off first, and climbing steeply disappeared into the eastern sky. Bertie and Tex followed, heading north and south, respectively.

Biggles spoke to Flight-Sergeant Smyth, who was standing by. 'Remember to smooth out our wheel tracks as soon as we're off,' he said. Then he called to Ginger: 'All right, let's get away. Make a careful note of anything that will serve as a landmark. The course is due west. We'll fly parallel some distance apart. If you see anything suspicious, or worth investigating, come across to me and wave—I'll follow you back to it. I shall keep you in sight; in the same way, you watch me. Let's go.'

The machines were soon in the air, heading west, with the oasis, a tiny island in an ocean of sand, receding astern. At fifteen thousand feet Biggles levelled out, and with a wave to his partner, turned a few points towards the south. Ginger moved north until the other machine was a mere speck in the sky, when he came back to his original westerly course. Throttling back to cruising speed he settled down to survey the landscape.

At first, all he could see was an endless expanse of sand, difficult to look at on account of the glare, stretching away to the infinite distance, colourless and without outline. Nowhere was there rest for the eye. There was no definite configuration, no scene to remember, nothing to break the eternal monotony of sand except occasional patches of camel-thorn, or small outcrops of what appeared to be grey rock. Over this picture of utter desolation hung an atmosphere of brooding, over-whelming solitude. Overhead, from a sky of gleaming steel, the sun struck down with bars of white heat, causing the rarefied air to quiver and the machine to rock as though in protest.

Ginger had flown over such forbidding territory before, but even so he was not immune from the feeling of depression it creates. Assailed by a sense of loneli-ness, as though he alone was left in a world that had died, he was glad that the other machine was there to remind him that this was not the case. Pulling down his smoked glasses over his eyes to offset the glare he flew on, subjecting the ground, methodically, section by section, to a close scrutiny. For some time it revealed nothing, but then a strange scar appeared, a trampled line of sand that came up from the south, to disappear again in the shimmering heat of the northern horizon. He soon realised what it was. The litter of tiny white gleaming objects that accompanied the trail he knew must be bones, human bones and camel bones, polished by years of sun and wind-blown sand. 'So that's the old caravan road, the ancient slave trail,' he mused. 'Poor devils.' It was an outstanding landmark, and he made careful note of it.

Some time later, on the fringe of an area furrowed by mightily curving dunes, as if a stormy ocean had suddenly been frozen, he saw another heap of bones—or, rather, an area of several square yards littered with them. Clearly, it marked the spot where a caravan, having left the trail, had met its fate, or perhaps had been wiped out by those fierce nomads of the desert, the veiled Toureg. Ginger marked down the spot, which formed another useful landmark in an area where land-marks were rare. He made a note of the time, to fix its position in relation to the oasis. This done, he glanced across at Biggles's machine, and having satisfied himself that it was there, still on its course, he went on, and soon afterwards came to the fringe of country broken by more extensive outcrops of rock, between which the camel-thorn grew in thick clumps, which suggested that although the country was still a wilderness there might be water deep down in the earth. Shortly afterwards Biggles came close and flew across his nose, waving the signal for return.

On the return journey the two machines for the most part flew together, although occasionally Biggles made a brief sortie, sometimes to the north and sometimes to the south. In this way they returned to the oasis, after what, to Ginger, had been a singularly uneventful flight. Landing, they taxied in to find that the other machines were already home. The pilots were waiting in the mess tent.

Biggles took them in turn, starting with Algy.

'See anything?' he asked crisply.

Algy shook his head. 'Not a thing.'

'What about you, Bertie?'

'I saw plenty of sand, but nothing else.'

Tex and Tug made similar negative reports.

Biggles rubbed his chin thoughtfully. 'We didn't see anything, either, except the old caravan route,' he said slowly. 'I was hoping we should find one of the missing machines so that by examination we might discover what forced it down. Between us we must have covered thousands of square miles of country. I don't understand it. To-morrow we'll try north-east and north-west—perhaps one of those districts will reveal something. If we draw blank again, I shall begin to think that my calculations were at fault. It isn't as though we were flying over wooded country; if the missing machines came down in this area we are bound to see them. It's very odd. If they didn't land, where did they go? Why did they leave the route? They certainly didn't land on it, or not in the four hundred miles of it which we've covered this morning.'

'They might have got off their course,' suggested Algy.

'I could believe that one might, but I'm dashed if I can imagine seven machines making the same mistake.'

'We may find them all in the same sector, one of the areas we haven't covered yet,' put in Ginger.

'If we do it will puzzle me still more,' declared Biggles. 'It will raise the question, why did seven machines leave the route at practically the same spot? Don't ask me to believe that the Higher Command would choose for a job like this pilots who are incapable of flying a simple compass course. In fact, I know they didn't, because Fred Gillson was flying one of the machines, a Rapide of British Overseas Airways, and he was a master pilot. No, there's something queer about this, something I don't understand. We'll have a spot of lunch, and perhaps do another patrol this evening.'

Biggles looked sharply at the tent entrance as Flight-Sergeant Smyth appeared. 'Yes, flight-sergeant, what is it?' he asked.

'A signal, sir, just in. I've decoded it.' The flight-sergeant passed a slip of paper.

Biggles looked at it. 'Good,' he said. 'This may give us a line. One of our machines, a Dragon*, wearing the identification letters GB-ZXL, left the West Coast

---

* De Havilland Dragon, a twin engined transport biplane.

at seven this morning. It must be well on its way by now, and should pass over here inside a couple of hours. General Demaurice is among the passengers; he's coming out to take over a contingent of the Free French*, so there will be trouble if the machine doesn't get through. We can escort it through this area. Ginger, come with me. We'll go to meet it. We'll take the same course as we did this morning, although we may have to fly a bit farther apart so that it won't slip by without our spotting it. Don't go far from the route, though. Algy, you stand by with Bertie; when you hear the Dragon coming, whether we are with it or not, take off and escort it over the eastern sector as far as your petrol will allow you to go. Flight-sergeant, you stand by the radio in case another message comes through. Come on, Ginger, we've no time to lose.'

In a few minutes the two machines were in the air again, climbing steeply for height and taking precisely the same course as they had taken earlier in the day except that Ginger went slightly farther to the north, and Biggles to the south, an arrangement which enabled the two machines to watch the air, not only on the exact route, but for several miles on either side of it, in case the Dragon should have deviated slightly from its compass course.

As he flew, Biggles kept his eyes on the atmosphere ahead for the oncoming machine. Occasionally, for the first half-hour, he saw Ginger in the distance, but from then on he saw no more of him. This did not perturb him, for it was now about noon, and although it could

* French troops still fighting against Germany and Italy after the occupation of France in 1940. They were led by General de Gaulle and the Free French Government operating in exile in London.

25

not be seen he knew that the usual deceptive heat-haze was affecting visibility.

Time passed, but still there was no sign of the Dragon, and Biggles' anxiety increased with each passing minute. Where could the machine be? He made fresh mental calculations, which only proved that his earlier ones had been right. If the Dragon had kept on its course at its normal cruising speed he should have met it before this.

When an hour had passed he knew beyond all shadow of doubt that one of two things must have happened. Either the Dragon had slipped past him in the haze, or, for some reason unknown, it had not reached the area of his patrol. He realised that there was a chance that Ginger had picked it up, and turned back to escort it, a possibility that was to some extent confirmed by the fact that there was no sign of Ginger's machine.

Perceiving that he was already running his petrol supply to fine limits Biggles turned for home, and in doing so had a good look at the ground. Instantly his nerves tingled with shock as he found himself staring at a wide outcrop of rock which he had not seen on his earlier flight, although had the rock been there he could not have failed to notice it. How could such a state of affairs have come about? There was only one answer to that question. He was not flying over the same course as he had flown earlier in the day. But according to his compass he *was* flying over the same course; he had never deviated more than a mile or two from it, a negligible distance in a country of such immense size.

Biggles thought swiftly. Obviously, something was wrong. He could not believe that his compass was at fault because compasses rarely go wrong, and, moreover, he had boxed* it carefully before starting for the oasis. Yet if his compass was right, how did he come to be flying over country that he had never seen before? This was a problem for which he could find no answer. The sun was of very little use to help him fix his position for it was practically overhead, so he took the only course left open to him, which was to climb higher in the hope of picking up a landmark which he had noted on his first flight.

By this time he was flying back over his course, or as near to it as he could judge without relying on his compass, but even so, it was not until he had climbed to twenty thousand feet that, with genuine relief, he saw, far away to the south-east, the caravan road. How it came to be where it was, or how he came to be so far away from it, he could not imagine. For the moment he was content to make for it, and from it get a rough idea of his position. The road ran due north and south. By cutting across it at right angles he would at least be on an easterly course, which was the one he desired to take him back to the oasis. And so it worked out. Half an hour later the oasis came into sight, and soon afterwards he was on the ground, shouting urgently for Algy as he jumped down.

Algy, and the others, came out at a run.

'Have you seen the Dragon?' asked Biggles crisply.

'Not a sign of it,' answered Algy. 'We've been standing here waiting for it ever since you took off.'

Biggles moistened his sun-dried lips. 'Ginger is back, of course?'

---

* Boxing a compass involves correctly calibrating the compass to suit each fully-equipped aircraft.

'No,' declared Algy, alarm in his voice. 'We haven't seen anything of him.'

Biggles stared. 'This is serious,' he said. 'I cut my petrol pretty fine. If Ginger isn't back inside ten minutes he'll be out of juice.'

'What can have happened to him—it isn't like him to do anything daft,' put in Tex.

'I've got an idea what's happened to him,' answered Biggles grimly. 'Let's get into the shade and I'll tell you. Flight-sergeant, check up my compass will you, and report to me in the mess tent.'

'An extraordinary thing happened to me this morning,' went on Biggles, when the officers had assembled in the tent. 'I lost my way, or rather, my compass took me to one place this morning, and at noon, although it registered the same course, to a different place. I ended up miles north of where I thought I was.'

'Your compass must be out of order—if you see what I mean,' remarked Bertie.

'Obviously,' returned Biggles.

At that moment the flight-sergeant appeared in the doorway. 'Your compass is in perfect order, sir,' he said.

'Are you *sure*?' Biggles' voice was pitched high with incredulity.

'Certain, sir, I checked it myself.'

For a few seconds Biggles looked astounded; then the light of understanding dawned in his eyes. 'By thunder!' he cried. 'I've got it! Someone is putting a magnetic beam up, to distort compass needles. It's been done before. It was put up to-day to upset the Dragon and take the pilot off his course. I'll bet he was lured off his course in the same direction as the other seven. Ginger and I ran into the beam and our compasses were affected at the same time. That's why I went astray. Now the beam is off, my compass is okay again.'

'If the beam has been turned off we can assume that the Dragon is a casualty,' put in Algy slowly.

Biggles drew a deep breath. 'I'm afraid you're right, but I'm not thinking only of that. If this compass business is really happening it introduces another new factor.'

'What do you mean?'

'Look at it like this. Early this morning there was no interference. A machine then left the West Coast. Shortly afterwards the magnetic influence was switched on. That's too much like clockwork to be accidental. It looks as if the Messerschmitts don't have to patrol; they *know* where and when they can find an aircraft on the route. They couldn't know that unless someone, somewhere, is tipping them off, probably with a short-wave radio. A person doing that needn't necessarily be at the terminus—he might be anywhere along the route. There is this about it. I now have a pretty good idea of the direction in which the missing machines disappeared—I can judge that from the error of my own compass. We shall probably find Ginger in the same locality, unless he discovered in time what was happening and tried to get back. There's just a chance that he landed to look at something, although I don't think that's likely. After I've had a bite of lunch I shall have to go out and look for him.'

'Alone?' queried Algy.

'Yes,' answered Biggles shortly. 'I don't feel like risking too many machines until we know for certain what is happening, and therefore what to expect.

29

Someone will have to stay here to carry on in case I don't come back, which is always on the boards.'

'Why not let me go?' suggested Algy.

'No.' Biggles was definite. 'I've been out in that direction and you haven't.'

'Where shall we look for you, if for any reason you don't get back?'

Biggles thought for a moment. 'I fancy Ginger is somewhere in the area north-west from here, between a hundred and two hundred miles distant. Your best plan would be to fly due west until you come to the caravan road; cross it, and then turn north. That's the way I shall go. You'll see a big outcrop of rock. I don't know how far it stretches—I didn't wait to see; but that, as near as I can tell you, is where I expect to find Ginger. If I'm not back in two hours you'll know I'm down, but give me until to-morrow morning before you start a search because I might land voluntarily, for some reason or other. I might have to go down to Ginger if I see him on the ground, or possibly the Dragon, although I shall await official confirmation that it has failed to arrive before I organize a serious search for it.' Biggles turned to Flight-Sergeant Smyth who was still waiting for instructions. 'Get my machine refuelled,' he ordered. 'Tell the mess waiter he can serve lunch. That's all.'

Over lunch, a frugal affair of bully beef, biscuits, tinned peaches and coffee, the matter was discussed in all its aspects, without any new light being thrown on the mystery. Ginger failed to put in an appearance. When, at four o'clock, there was still no sign of him, Biggles took off and headed west. The sun, long past its zenith, was sinking in the same direction.

Reaching the broken country beyond the caravan

30

road Biggles turned sharply north, to find that the rocks grew bolder, sometimes running up to small, jagged hills, with gullies filled with drift sand between them. This sand he eyed with deep suspicion, for experience had taught him its peculiar properties. In some places, he knew, the grains of sand would have packed down like concrete, hard enough to carry a heavy vehicle; in other places it would be as soft as liquid mud, a death trap to any vehicle that tried to cross it—a phenomenon due to the force and direction of the wind when the sand was deposited. Barren and desolate, worse country would have been hard to imagine, and Biggles had to fly low in order to distinguish details.

He was following a smooth, sandy gully, hemmed in by gaunt, sun-scorched rocks, rising in places to a fair height, when he came suddenly upon the object of his quest. There, in the middle of the gully, stood the Spitfire, apparently undamaged, and abandoned. There was no sign of movement. The airscrew was stationary.

Biggles was amazed. Although he was looking for the aircraft, and expected to find it, he had not supposed that he would discover it in such peculiar circumstances. He would not have been surprised to find that it had crashed, nor would he have been astonished had Ginger been standing beside it. What he could not understand was why, if the machine was in order, as it appeared to be, it had been abandoned. The sand seemed to be firm enough, judging from the shallow wheel tracks.

With the fear of soft sand still in his mind he did not land at once, but circled the stationary machine at a height of not more than fifty feet, to make sure that the wheels were fully visible—that they had not sunk into the sand. Satisfied that they had not, he landed, and taxied to the deserted aircraft.

Jumping down from his own machine he ran over to it. He had a horror that he might find Ginger dead, or seriously hurt, in the cockpit, but it was empty. For a moment he started at it blankly, not knowing what to think. He could not find a bullet hole, or a mark of any sort, to account for the landing. The petrol gauge revealed that the tank was still half full. He even tried the engine, and finding it in perfect order, switched off again. Standing up, he surveyed the sterile landscape around him.

'Ginger!' he shouted. And then again, 'Hi, Ginger!'

But there was no reply. Silence, the silence of death, took possession of the melancholy scene.

Chapter 3
What Happened to Ginger

Ginger, out over the desert, like Biggles devoted most of his attention to the sky ahead, hoping to see the oncoming Dragon. Also like his leader, he had no reason to suppose that his compass was not functioning perfectly. It was not until he happened to glance at his watch, on the instrument panel, and then at the ground below, that the first dim suspicion that something was wrong entered his head. He looked down fully expecting to see the scattered heap of white bones that he had noted on his previous flight. It was a conspicuous landmark, and according to the time shown by his watch it should not merely have been in sight, but underneath him. There was no sign of any bones. Moreover, the terrain looked strange—not that he paid a great deal of attention to this because the desert was so much alike that he felt he might easily be mistaken. Yet where were the bones? He could see the ground for many miles in every direction, but there was nothing remotely resembling a heap of bones.

He happened to be wearing his wrist watch, so his next move was to check it with the watch on the instrument board. Both watches registered the same time, which puzzled him still more, for as he had flown over the same course, at the same speed, for the same length of time as before, the bones, he thought, *must* be there.

He slipped off five thousand feet of height and studied the ground closely. There were no bones, and the conviction grew on him that he had never seen that particular stretch of wilderness before. There were too many rocks. Over his starboard bow there was an absolute jumble of them, biggish rocks, too. Such faith had he in his instruments that not for an instant did he suspect the truth—that his compass was out of order. After all, there was no reason why he should suspect such a thing. He looked across to the left. He could see no sign of Biggles' machine, but noted that the heat haze was exceptionally bad. The heat, even in his cockpit, was terrific.

Concerned, but not in any way alarmed, he flew on, and as he flew he made a careful reconnaissance of the grey rocks on his right. At one point, far away, something flashed. Pushing up his sun goggles he saw a quivering point of white light among the rocks. Only three things, he knew, could flash like that in the desert. One was water, another, polished metal, and the other, glass. He knew it could not be water or there would be vegetation, probably palms. He did not think it could be metal because the only metal likely to be in such a place was a weapon of some sort, carried by an Arab, in which case the point of light would not be constant. That left only glass. It looked like glass. He had seen plenty of broken glass winking at him in districts where there were human beings. Indeed, in Egypt he had seen Biggles follow a trail by such points of light, the flashes there being made by empty bottles thrown away by thirsty travellers.

His curiosity aroused he turned towards the object. He realized that this was taking him farther away from Biggles, but he thought he was justified. In any case, he expected no difficulty in returning to Biggles after he had ascertained what it was that could flash in a place where such a thing was hardly to be expected. Putting his nose down, both for speed and in order to lose more height, he raced towards the spot, and in five minutes was circling low over it.

He had only to look once to see what it was. Piled up against the base of a low but sheer face of rock, was an aircraft. The flashing light had been caused by its shattered windscreen. There was no sign of life, and although he flew low over it several times trying to make out the registration letters, he could not, because both wings and fuselage were crumpled. Nor could he be sure of the type. The only letter he could read was G, which told him that the aircraft was a British civil plane, evidently one of the missing machines which Biggles was so anxious to locate. A ghastly thought struck him. Could it be the Dragon they were out to escort? Were they too late after all? Were there, in that crumpled cabin, injured men, perhaps dying of thirst?

This possibility threw his brain into a turmoil. What ought he to do? Was he justified in calling Biggles on the radio? He wasn't sure. He knew Biggles was most anxious that the radio should not be used if it could possibly be avoided. Should he try to find Biggles? Even if he succeeded, he had no way of conveying the information he possessed. Biggles would probably return to the base, and it would be hours before they could get back. Ginger did, in fact, turn towards the south, and fly a little way, hoping to see Biggles; but then it struck him that he might not be able to find the crashed machine again; it would certainly be no easy matter, lying as it did in a shapeless wilderness of rock.

Worried, Ginger swung round and raced back to the wreck. He could see clearly what had happened. Behind the rock there was a small, fairly level area of sand. Wheel tracks showed that the pilot had tried to get down on it, but had been unable to pull up before colliding head-on with the cliff. Had the sand area been larger Ginger would have felt inclined to risk a landing; but the area was too small; if a comparatively slow commercial machine could not get in, what chance had he, in a Spitfire? It struck him that the pilot must have been hard pressed to attempt a landing in such a place. But uppermost in his mind was the horror that someone might still be alive in the wreck, too badly injured to move. It made the thought of flying away abhorrent to him. Clearly, at all costs—and he was well aware of the risks—he must try to get down to satisfy himself that the machine was really abandoned.

Climbing a little, and circling, he soon found what he sought—a long, level area of sand. It was not entirely what he would have wished, for it had length without breadth, forming, as it were, the base of a long, rock-girt gully. But still, he reflected, there was no wind to fix the direction of landing, so he had the full length of the gully to get in. His greatest fear was that the sand might be soft enough to clog his wheels and pitch him on his nose, or failing that, prevent him from getting off again. There was no way of determining this from the air; it was a risk he would have to take, and he prepared to take it.

First he took the precaution of noting carefully the direction of the crash in relation to the gully, for they were about five hundred yards apart; then, lining up with his landing ground, he cut the engine and glided down. To do him justice, he was fully aware of the risks he was taking, but he thought the circumstances justified them. Concentrating absolutely on his perilous task, he flattened out, held off as long as he dare, and

36

then—holding his breath in his anxiety—he allowed the machine to settle down. His mouth went dry as the wheels touched, but an instant later he was breathing freely again as the Spitfire ran on to a perfectly smooth landing, finishing its run almost in the middle of the gully.

Switching off his engine, he jumped down and stood for a moment stretching his cramped muscles while he regarded the scene around him. His first impression was one of heat. It was appalling, as though he had landed in an oven. The air, the sand and the rock all quivered as the sun's fierce lances struck into them. The second thing was the silence, an unimaginable silence, a silence so profound that every sound he made was magnified a hundredfold. There was not a sign of life—not an insect, not a blade of grass. Even the hardy camel-thorn had found the spot detestable.

In such a place a man would soon lose his reason, thought Ginger, as, after throwing off his jacket, which he found unbearable, he walked quickly in the direction of the wreck. When he had gone about a hundred yards he remembered Biggles' order about not moving without a water-bottle, and he hesitated in his stride, undecided whether to return to the machine for it or to go on without it. He decided to go on. After all, he mused, it was only a short distance to the wreck, and he would be back at his own machine in a few minutes. Nothing could happen in that time. It was not as though he were going on a journey. Thus he thought, naturally, perhaps, but in acting as he did he broke the first rule of desert travel.

It did not take him long to reach the machine. He approached it with misgivings, afraid of what the cabin might hold. While still a short distance away he saw that it was not the Dragon, but a similar type, a Rapide*, carrying the registration letters G—VDH. The crash had been a bad one, the forward part of the aircraft having been badly buckled, and consequently he breathed a sigh of relief when he found the cabin empty. But three of the passengers, or crew, had not gone far. Close at hand were three heaps of sand, side by side, obviously graves, but there was no mark to show who the victims were. Ginger considered the pathetic heaps gloomily before returning to the machine. There was nothing in it of interest. There was no luggage. Even the pilot and engine log-books had been taken from their usual compartment in the cockpit. Further examination revealed the reason why the machine had attempted to land. Across the nose, and also through the tail, were unmistakable bullet holes, and Ginger's face set in hard lines when he realized that the defenceless machine had been shot down. A number of questions automatically arose. In the first place, why was the machine so far off its track? For off its compass course it most certainly was. Enemy aircraft must have done the shooting, but where were the surviving passengers? Had they buried their dead and then set off on a hopeless march towards civilization?

Ginger found the answers to some of these questions in the sand. The sand on the graves had been patted smooth by a spade, or similar implement. Such a tool would not be carried by the aircraft. The absence of footprints leading away from the crash puzzled him, but he soon found a clue which solved that particular problem. A set of wheel tracks told the story. A wheeled vehicle, keeping close to the face of the low cliff, had

---

* De Havilland Dragon Rapide, a twin-engined biplane.

38

come almost to the crash. It had turned, and then gone away in the direction from which it had come—that is, towards the north.

The tragic story was now fairly plain to read. The machine, which for some unexplained reason had got off its course, had been shot down. The pilot, or pilots, responsible for shooting it down had informed their base, noting the spot where the crash had occurred, with the result that a vehicle had been sent out to examine it. Three passengers had perished. Their enemies had buried them and taken the survivors away. That was all, and as far as Ginger was concerned it was enough. The sooner Biggles knew about his discovery the better. In any case, he was already finding the heat more than he could comfortably bear. Pondering on the tragedy, he set off on the return journey to the Spitfire.

He had gone about half-way when he heard a sound that caused him to pull up short. It was the drone of an aircraft, still a long way off, but approaching, and the shrill whine of it told him that it was running on full throttle. At first he assumed, naturally, that it was Biggles, but as he stood listening his expression became one of mixed astonishment and alarm. There was more than one aircraft—or at any rate more than one engine. Then, as he stood staring in the direction of the sound, there came another, one that turned his lips dry with apprehension. It was the vicious grunt of multiple machine-guns.

He dived for cover, for he was standing in the open and did not want to be seen, as a Dragon suddenly took shape in the haze. It was flying low, running tail up on full throttle and turning from side to side as the pilot tried desperately to escape the fire of three fighters that kept him close company. It did not need the swastikas that decorated them to tell Ginger what they were. Their shape was enough. They were Messerschmitts.

As soon as he realized what was happening he threw discretion to the winds and raced like a madman towards his Spitfire, but before he had gone fifty yards he knew he would be too late. The one-sided running fight had swept over him, and a jagged escarpment hid it from view. The machine-gunning ended abruptly, and the roar of engines seemed suddenly to diminish in volume.

Although he could not see, Ginger could visualize the picture. The British pilot, realizing the futility of trying to escape from its attackers, was trying to land, and so save the lives of his passengers. It was the only sensible thing to do.

And then, as Ginger stood staring white-faced in the direction in which the machines had disappeared, came a sound which, once heard, is never forgotten. It was the splintering crackle of a crashing aeroplane. The distance he judged to be not more than four or five miles away.

For a few seconds the drone of the Messerschmitts continued, as, no doubt, they circled round the remains of the Dragon; then the sound faded swiftly, and silence once more settled over the desert.

Now Ginger did what was perhaps a natural thing, but a foolish one—as he realized later. Acting on the spur of the moment, without stopping to think, he dashed up the rock escarpment which hid the tragedy from view. Panting and gasping, for the heat of the rock was terrific, he reached the top, only to discover that another ridge, not more than a hundred yards away, still hid what he was so anxious to see. So upset was he that he was only subconsciously aware of the blinding heat as he ran on to the ridge, again to discover that an even higher ridge was in front of him.

He pulled up short, suddenly aware of the folly of what he was doing. Already he was hot, thirsty and exhausted from emotion and violent movement in such an atmosphere. He realized that he had been foolish to leave the Spitfire without his water-bottle. He needed a drink—badly. He could not see the Spitfire from where he stood, but he knew where it was—or thought he did—and made a bee-line towards the spot.

For a time he walked confidently, and it was only when he found himself face to face with a curiously shaped mass of rock that he experienced his first twinge of uneasiness. He knew that he had never seen that particular rock before; it was too striking to be overlooked. Still, he was not alarmed, but simply annoyed with himself for carelessness which resulted in a loss of valuable time.

Turning slightly towards a rock which he thought he recognized, he walked on, only to discover that he had been mistaken. It was not the rock he had supposed. He began to hurry now, keeping a sharp lookout for something that he could recognize. But there was nothing, and irritation began to give way to fear. Fragments of Biggles' warning drifted into his memory, such pieces as 'shrivelling like an autumn leaf.'

He had been following a shallow valley between the rocks, and it now struck him that if he climbed one of the highest rocks he ought to be able to see his machine or the crashed Rapide. Choosing an eminence, he clambered to the summit—not without difficulty, for it was hot enough to burn his hands. The sight that met his eyes horrified him. On all sides stretched a wilderness of rock and sand, colourless, shapeless, hideous in its utter lifelessness.

He discovered that his mouth had turned bricky dry, and for once he nearly gave way to panic. No experience in the air had ever filled him with such fear. His legs seemed to go weak under him. Slowly, for he was terrified now of hurting himself and thus making his plight worse, he descended the rock and ran to the next one, which he thought was a trifle higher. Looking round frantically, he was faced with the same scene as before. It all looked alike. Rock and sand . . . sand and rock, more sand, more rock.

Running, he began to retrace his footsteps—or so he thought—to the escarpment, and was presently overjoyed to find his own footprints in the soft sand. He followed them confidently, feeling sure that they would take him back to the crash. Instead they brought him back to the same place. He had walked in a circle. With growing horror in his heart he realized that he was lost, and he stood still for a moment to get control of his racing brain.

Bitterly now he repented his rash behaviour—not that it did any good. The silence really frightened him. It was something beyond the imagination. It seemed to beat in his ears. A falling pebble made a noise like an avalanche. He trudged on through a never-altering world. All he could see was rock and sand, except, above him, a dome of burnished steel. Time passed; how long he did not know. He was not concerned with time. All he wanted was the Spitfire, and the water that was in his water-bottle. The idea of water was fast becoming a mania. Very soon it was torture. Several times he climbed rocks, but they were all too low to give him a clear view. The loneliness and the silence became unbearable, and he began to shout for the sake of hearing a human voice. He could no longer look at the sky; it had become the open door of a furnace. He put his hands on his head, which was beginning to ache. He no longer perspired, for the searing heat snatched away any moisture as soon as it was formed. He felt that his body was being dried up—as Biggles had said—like a shrivelled leaf.

Hopelessness took him in its grip. He knew he was wandering in circles, but he had ceased to care. All he wanted to do was drink. His skin began to smart. His feet were on fire. His tongue was like a piece of dried leather in his mouth. Sand gritted between his teeth. The rocks began to sway, to recede, then rush at him. Rock and sand. It was always the same. A white haze began to close in on him. Presently it turned orange. He didn't care. He didn't care about anything. He could only think of one thing—water.

He walked on, muttering. The rocks became monsters, marching beside him. He shouted to scare them away, but they took no notice. He saw Biggles sitting on one, but when he got to it it was only another rock. Beyond, he saw a line of blue water, with little flecks of white light dancing on it. It was so blue that it dazzled him. Shouting, he ran towards it, but it was always the same distance away, and it took his reeling brain some little time to realize that it was not there. He began to laugh. What did it matter which way he went? All ways were the same in this cauldron. More monsters were coming towards him. He rushed at them and beat at them with his fists. He saw blood on his knuckles, but he felt no pain. The sky turned red. Everything turned red. The sand seemed to be laughing at him. He hated it, and in his rage he knelt down and thumped it. It only laughed all the louder. The voice sounded very real. He tried to shout, but he could only croak.

44

Chapter 4
Shadows In The Night

Suddenly Ginger became conscious that he was drinking; that water, cool, refreshing water, was splashing on his face. He knew, of course, that it wasn't true, but he didn't mind that. It was the most wonderful sensation he had ever known, and he only wanted it to go on for ever. His great fear was that it would stop; and, surely enough, it did stop. Opening his eyes, he found himself gazing into the concerned face of his leader.

'All right, take it easy,' said Biggles.

'You were—just about—in time,' gasped Ginger.

'And you, my lad, have had better luck than you deserve.' Compassion faded suddenly from Biggles' face; the muscles of his jaws tightened. 'I seem to remember making an order about all ranks carrying water-bottles,' he said in a voice as brittle as cracking ice. 'If we were within striking distance of a service depôt I'd put you under close arrest for breaking orders. As it is, if you feel able to move, we'd better see about getting out of this sun-smitten dustbin. It will be dark before we get back as it is.'

Ginger staggered to his feet. 'Sorry, sir,' he said contritely.

'So you thundering well ought to be,' returned Biggles grimly. 'Why did you land in the first place?'

'I saw a crashed aircraft, and came down to see if there was anyone in it.'

45

Biggles started. 'A crash? Where?'

Ginger shrugged his shoulders helplessly. 'I don't know, but it can't be far away. Do you know where my machine is?'

'Yes, I landed by it. I saw it from some way off and went straight to it.'

'That's probably why you didn't see the crash; it's lying close up against a cliff. It's a Rapide. It was the flash of broken glass that took me to it. Somehow I'd got off my course.'

'I can't blame you for that,' answered Biggles. 'I had the same experience. Magnetic interference was put up to affect our compasses—or rather to affect the compass of the Dragon.'

'Great Scott! I'd almost forgotten,' declared Ginger. 'You're dead right. The Dragon came this way. It was being attacked by three Messerschmitts. They roared right over me, but I reckon they were too concerned with their own affairs to see me. That's what started my trouble. I heard a machine crash some way off, and instead of returning to my Spitfire I climbed an escarpment to see if I could see the crash. I couldn't see it, though. It was in going back to my machine that I lost my way.'

Biggles looked amazed at this recital—as he had every reason to. He was silent for a moment.

'We shall have to get all these facts in line,' he said presently. 'Assuming that, like me, you had compass trouble, I came out to look for you. I found your machine and landed by it. I was a bit worried to find you weren't with it. I was wondering where you could have gone when I heard someone laughing and shouting—'

'You *heard* me—from the Spitfires?'

'Certainly.'

Ginger stared. 'Then I must have been wandering about close to my machine?'

'I don't know about that,' replied Biggles. 'All I can tell you is the Spitfires are just behind those rocks on the left—less than a hundred yards away.'

'Just imagine it,' said Ginger bitterly. 'I might have passed out from thirst within a hundred yards of water.'

'That's how it happens,' said Biggles seriously. 'Don't say I didn't warn you. But let's get to the machines. Thank goodness the heat isn't quite so fierce now the sun is going down.'

Dusk was, in fact, advancing swiftly across the shimmering waste as the sun sank in a final blaze of crimson glory. There was just time to walk to the Spitfires, make a trip to the crashed Rapide, and return, before complete darkness descended on the wilderness. The heat, as Biggles had remarked, was less fierce; but the atmosphere was stifling as every rock, and every grain of sand, continued to radiate the heat it had absorbed during the day.

Biggles leaned against the fuselage of his machine and lit a cigarette. 'I don't feel like taking off in this black-out,' he told Ginger. 'Nor do I feel like risking a night flight across the desert with a compass that isn't entirely to be relied on. We're in no particular hurry. The moon will be up in an hour, so we may as well wait for it. I've some thinking to do, and I can do that as well here as anywhere. Tell me, in which direction was the Dragon flying when you last saw it—presumably the sound of the crash came from the same direction?'

'Yes,' answered Ginger. 'It was over there.' He pointed to the escarpment, its jagged ridge boldly silhouetted against the starlit heavens. 'I couldn't swear how far it was away, because sounds are so deceptive here, but I wouldn't put it at more than five miles. What are you thinking of doing?'

'I was wondering if we should try to find it.'

'Not for me,' declared Ginger. 'I've had one go at that sort of thing. You got me out of the frying-pan, and I don't want to fall in it again.'

'There's less risk of that at night, when you have stars to guide—Great Scott! What's that?'

For a little while both Biggles and Ginger stood staring in the direction of the escarpment, beyond which a glowing finger of radiance, straight as a ruler, was moving slowly across the sky.

'It's a searchlight,' declared Ginger.

'If it is, then it's a dickens of a long way away,' returned Biggles. 'Whatever it is, it's mobile. Look at the base of it—you can see it moving along the rock . . . that's queer, it's stopped now. I think I know what it is. It's the headlight of a car, deflected upwards.'

'A car!' said Ginger incredulously. 'A car—here—in the desert?'

'You haven't forgotten that a car came out to the crashed Rapide—or a vehicle of some sort? It was not one of ours; therefore it must have belonged to the enemy. Whoever shot the Rapide down would report where it had crashed. Unless I'm mistaken, the same thing is happening now. A car is on its way to the crashed Dragon. If it can't get right up to it, no doubt it will go as close as possible; the people in it can walk the rest of the way. This is an opportunity to learn something definite, and I don't feel inclined to miss it. Our machines will be safe enough here—unless the car

48

comes this way, which seems unlikely. Anyway, it's a risk worth taking.'

With Ginger's water-bottle slung over his shoulder, Biggles started off in a direct line towards the light, which still appeared as a faint, slender beam, like a distant searchlight. From the top of the escarpment a good deal more of it could be seen—the lower part, which descended to a point.

'No British forces are operating in this district, so whoever is putting that beam up must be an enemy,' said Biggles thoughtfully, as he stood staring at it.

'How far away do you think it is?'

'That's impossible to tell, because we don't know the strength of the beam. It might be a weak one fairly close, or a powerful one a long way off. What puzzles me is why it is turned upwards. It can't be looking for aircraft.'

'It could be a signal, a signpost, so to speak, for airmen.'

'Possibly, but unlikely, for there seems to be no reason why enemy aircraft should operate at night.' Biggles laughed shortly. 'What a fool I am—the heat must have made me dense. The beam *is* a signpost, probably a rallying point, for people out in the desert on foot looking for the crashed Dragon. That, I think, is the most likely answer. Let's go on for a bit; maybe we shall see something. Speak quietly, and make no more noise than you can prevent, because we're approaching a danger zone, and sound travels a long way in the desert.'

They went on in silence, climbed the ridge that had baffled Ginger, and the one beyond it, which they discovered dropped sheer for about forty feet to a lower level of sand, generously sprinkled with broken rock.

In the deceptive starlight they nearly stepped over the edge before they realized how steep was the drop. They went a little way to the right hoping to find a way down, and finding none, tried the left; but the cliff—for they were on the lip of what might best be described as a low cliff—seemed to continue for some distance. There were one or two places where a descent appeared possible, and once Ginger moved forward with that object in mind; but Biggles held him back.

'I'm not going to risk it,' he said in a low voice. 'This desert rock isn't to be trusted; wind and sun make it friable; if it broke away and let us down with a bump we might hurt ourselves. If we were nearer home I wouldn't hesitate, but this is no place for even a minor injury—a sprained ankle, for instance. We're some way from the machines, too. But here comes the moon. Let's try to get a line on the light; if we can do that we may be able to check up in daylight.' So saying, Biggles lay flat and using his hands to mask the surrounding scenery, focused his attention on the foot of the beam.

Following his example, Ginger made out what appeared to be three successive ranges of low hills which, from their serrated ridges, were obviously stark rock. The light sprang up from behind the farthest, which he estimated to be not less than twelve miles away. He tried to photograph the silhouette of the rocks in line with the beam on his brain, this being made possible by certain salient features. In the first range there was a mass of rock that took the form of a frog, and behind it a group of four small pinnacles that might have been the spires of a cathedral. These were near enough in line with the beam to fix its position should the light be turned out, and he mentioned this to Biggles, who agreed, but reminded him that when they had first seen the light it had been moving, which proved that it was not constant.

The moon, nearly full, was now clear of the horizon, and cast a pale blue radiance over the wilderness. It was not yet light enough to read a newspaper, as the saying is, but it was possible to see clearly for a considerable distance; and if the lifeless scene had been depressing by day, thought Ginger, it was a hundred times worse at night.

He was about to rise when from somewhere—it was impossible to say how far away—there came a sound, a noise so slight that in the ordinary way it might well have passed unnoticed. It was as though a small piece of rock had struck against another.

Biggles' hand closed on Ginger's arm. 'Don't move,' he breathed.

Ginger, his muscles now taut, lay motionless, his eyes probing the direction from which he thought the sound had come, which was on the lower level to the right of where he lay. He stared and stared until the rocks appeared to take shape and move—not an uncommon reaction in darkness when nerves are strained. Moving his head slightly until his mouth was close to Biggles' ear, he whispered, 'Perhaps it was a jackal.'

Biggles shook his head. 'Nothing lives in this sort of desert.'

Another rock clicked, nearer this time, and Biggles hissed a warning.

Staring again at the lower level, Ginger saw that a group of what appeared to be shadows was moving silently towards them. Very soon they took shape, and it was possible to distinguish men and camels. There were six camels carrying riders, and a number of men walking behind them. Two of the camel riders rode side by side a little in advance of the rest of the party. The other four camels moved noiselessly in single file. Magnified by the flat background behind them they were huge, distorted, more like strange spirits of the desert than living creatures. They came on, heading obliquely towards the distant light. When the two leaders were quite close a voice spoke, suddenly, and the sound was so unexpected and so clear that Ginger stiffened with shock. But it was not only the actual sound that shook him; it was the language that the speaker had used.

Speaking in German, he had said in a harsh tone of voice: 'I'll tell these young fools of mine to let machines get farther in, in future, before they shoot them down. It's a good thing you know this country as well as you do, Pallini.'

A voice answered haltingly in the same language: 'Yes, Hauptmann* von Zoyton, it is a long way again. It was near here that the last machine was brought down. Fortunately I know every inch of the country, but it is always a good thing to have a light to march on. It makes it easier.'

It was now possible to see that both riders wore uniforms, although it was not easy to make out the details. Ginger watched them go past, with the words still ringing in his ears. Then the second part of the caravan drew in line. It comprised, first, the four camels, but this time the riders seemed to have their bodies wrapped in ragged sheets which reached up to their mouths, leaving only the eyes exposed. Rifle barrels projected high above their shoulders. Behind, strid-

---

* German rank equivalent to Captain.

52

ing on sandalled feet, were four other men similarly dressed, acting, it seemed, as an escort for five men who walked together in a dejected little group. Four were civilians and the other an officer, a heavily-built man with a square-cut black beard. Ginger caught the flash of gold braid on his sleeves and shoulders. These, too, passed on, and soon the entire caravan had merged as mysteriously as it had appeared into the vague shadows of the nearest range of hills.

Biggles neither moved nor spoke for a good five minutes after the party had disappeared. When he did speak his voice was the merest whisper.

'Very interesting,' he murmured. 'We're learning quite a lot.'

'Who did you make them out to be?' asked Ginger.

'Of the two fellows in front, one was a German and the other Italian. The Italian, whom the other called Pallini, was probably a local political officer—that would account for his knowing the country. His companion, you will remember, he called von Zoyton. It may not be the same man, but there has been a lot of talk up in the Western Desert about a star-turn pilot named von Zoyton—he commands a Messerschmitt *jagdstaffel**, and has some sort of stunt, a trick turn, they say, that has enabled him to pile up a big score of victories. I'm inclined to think it must be the same chap, sent down here for the express purpose of closing our trans-continental air route. The other mounted fellows, judging by their veils, were Toureg. There were also some Toureg on foot. The five people with them were prisoners, the passengers of the Dragon, on their

---

* A hunting group of German fighter planes. A staffel consisted of twelve planes.

way, no doubt, to the enemy camp. The beam was put up as a guide.'

'You seem very sure of that,' said Ginger curiously.

'I'm certain of it,' declared Biggles. 'You see, the fellow with the black beard was General Demaurice. I've never seen him in the flesh before, but I recognized him from photographs.'

'Is he an important man?'

'Very.'

'Then why didn't we attempt a rescue? We had the whole outfit stone cold. They had no idea we were here.'

'All right; don't get worked up,' replied Biggles quietly. 'It was neither the time nor place for a rescue. To start with, they were forty feet below us, and to break our legs by jumping down would have been silly. Suppose we had got the prisoners, what could we have done with them? We couldn't fly five passengers in two Spits, and they certainly couldn't have walked to Salima Oasis.'

'We could have fetched the Whitley from Karga.'

'Long before we could have got it here the Messerschmitts would have been out looking for us. Don't suppose I didn't contemplate a rescue, but it seemed to me one of those occasions when restraint was the better part of valour. Don't worry, our turn will come. We're doing fine. We know definitely that enemy machines are operating in the desert, and the approximate direction of their base. The only thing we have to reproach ourselves about is the loss of the Dragon, although now we know the technique that is being employed we ought to be able to prevent such a thing from happening again. Cruising about the desert with a compass that is liable to go gaga at any moment is,

I must admit, definitely disconcerting; it means that we shall have to check up constantly on landmarks—such as they are.'

'How about the Messerschmitts—why aren't their compasses upset at the same time?'

Biggles thought for a moment. 'There may be several answers to that,' he answered slowly. 'Their compasses may be specially insulated, or it may be they don't take off until the beam is switched off. The object of the beam seems to be to bring machines flying over the route nearer to the German base, to save the enemy from making long journeys in surface vehicles to the scene of a crash.'

'Why do they want to visit the crash, anyway?'

'To collect any mails or dispatches that are on board.'

'Of course, I'd forgotten that.' Ginger stood up. 'As nothing more is likely to happen to-night we may as well be getting back.'

'Not so fast,' answered Biggles. 'We can't take off yet, or the noise of our engines will be heard by von Zoyton and his party. We don't want them to know we're about. Still, we may as well get back to the machines.'

Biggles got up and led the way back to where the two Spitfires were standing side by side, looking strangely out of place in such a setting. He squatted down on the still warm sand and allowed a full hour to pass before he climbed into his cockpit. As he told Ginger, he had plenty to think about and plans to make. But at length, satisfied that the desert raiders were out of earshot, he started his engine. Ginger did the same. The machines took off together and cruised back to the oasis, which was reached without mishap, to find the others already making arrangements for a search as soon as it was light.

'Thank goodness you're back,' muttered Algy. 'At the rate we were going there would soon have been no squadron left,' he continued, inclined to be critical in his relief. 'What's going on?'

'Sit down, and I'll tell you,' answered Biggles, and gave the others a concise account of what had happened.

Tug Carrington made a pretence of spitting on his hands. 'That's grand,' he declared, balancing himself on his toes and making feints at imaginary enemies. 'Now we know where they are we can go over and shoot them up.'

'Tug, you always were a simple-minded fellow,' returned Biggles sadly. 'As you know, I'm all for direct methods when they are possible, but there are certain arguments against your plan that I can't ignore. To start with, there is no guarantee we should locate the enemy's base—you can be pretty certain it's well camouflaged—whereas they would certainly see us. It is, therefore, far more likely that we should merely reveal our presence without serving any useful purpose. When we strike we want to hit the blighters, and hit them hard, and we shall only do that by being sure of our ground. Make no mistake; if von Zoyton is here with his *jagdstaffel*, we shan't find them easy meat. They had a reputation in Libya. No, I think the situation calls for stratagem.' Biggles smiled at Algy. 'I wonder if we could pull off the old trap trick?'

'Which one?' asked Algy, grinning. 'There were several varieties, if you remember?'

'The decoy.'

'We might try it. But what shall we use for bait?'

'The Whitley.'

'You must think von Zoyton is a fool. He wouldn't be tricked by that.'

'I wasn't thinking of sending it through in its present war paint. By washing out the ring markings, and giving it a set of identification letters, we could make it look like a civil machine. Let's try it. After all, it can but fail. Remember, the Boches don't know we're here. Bertie, you've had a quiet day. Do you feel like playing mouse in a little game of cat-and-mouse?'

Bertie polished his eyeglass industriously. 'Absolutely, old top,' he agreed. 'I'll play any part you like, you bet I will, if it means hitting von what's-his-name a wallop.'

'That's fine,' returned Biggles. 'This is what you have to do. Go to Karga. Tell Angus what's in the wind. Get all hands working on the Whitley, making it look as much like a civil machine as possible. Then, at dawn, take off and fly it through. You'll have to work fast. Come over here at about ten thousand, and then head for the danger zone.'

'Here, I say, what about some guns?' protested Bertie.

'You can stick as many guns in as you like, as far as I'm concerned,' granted Biggles. 'Angus will provide you with some gunners. But don't go fooling about. You're not supposed to fight. Leave that to us. We shall be upstairs, waiting for the Messerschmitts. Angus can send out a radio signal that you're on your way. If von Zoyton picks it up he'll soon be after you. Is that clear?'

'Absolutely, yes, absolutely,' murmured Bertie. 'What fun! Here I go. See you in the morning. Cheerio, and so forth.'

The others watched him take off and disappear in the starry sky towards the east.

Biggles turned away. 'All right, chaps, go to bed,' he ordered. 'We have a busy day in front of us tomorrow.'

Chapter 5
The Decoy

The next morning, while the sky was turning from pink to eggshell blue and the palms were nodding in the dawn-wind, Flight-Sergeant Smyth reported to Biggles, who, with the four pilots who remained with him, was at breakfast.

'Signal, sir, from Karga. British aircraft, G-UROK is on its way to the West Coast,' he reported.

'Good. Stand by for further signals.'

The flight-sergeant saluted and retired.

'All right, you chaps, there's no hurry,' went on Biggles, lighting a cigarette. 'It will be some time before Bertie gets to the danger zone. I'll just run over the programme again to make sure you understand the scheme—we don't want any mistakes. What eventually happens must, of course, largely depend on how many machines von Zoyton sends up against the Whitley— assuming that he will try to stop it. As he sent three against the Dragon— Ginger saw only three, you remember—he'll probably use the same number again. Three fighters certainly ought to be enough for one commercial aircraft, which he will, we hope, take the Whitley to be. We shall meet the Whitley about fifty miles or so east of here. I shall take up a position immediately above it, at twenty thousand, with Ginger and Tug. Algy, you'll take Tex with you and sit up at twenty-five thousand, a trifle to the north, always keeping us, and the Whitley, in sight. We shall take on

59

the Messerschmitts if they turn up. Your job, with Tex, is to see that none of them get home—cut off anyone who tries. That, I am well aware, sounds optimistic, and we may not be able to do it; but we must try, because if we can prevent any of the enemy from getting back it will still leave all the cards in our hands. It will be von Zoyton's turn to start worrying—wondering what happened to *his* machines. If any of his machines do get back it will be open war in future, because he'll know there's a British squadron on the job. Speaking from experience, I should say that when the Messerschmitts go for the Whitley they won't look at anything else, for the simple reason, not having had any opposition before, they won't look for it this time. We should be on them before they know we're about—perhaps get one or two at the first crack. If a combat starts, you, Algy, and Tex, will get between the Nazis and home, although as I said just now, much is bound to depend on how many of them there are, if, in fact, they show up. If they don't, well, no harm will have been done, and we shall have to think of something else. And now, if that's clear, we may as well get ready to move off. We'll leave the ground in half an hour; that will give Bertie time to get to our area. Algy and Tex will take off first and go straight up topsides; the rest of us will follow.' Biggles finished his coffee, stamped his cigarette end into the sandy floor, and led the way to where the machines were parked under camouflage netting.

One by one they were dragged clear. Algy and Tex climbed into their seats. Engines sprang to life, and the machines taxied out to the clear sand. In a few minutes they were in the air, with their wheels, no longer required, tucked away. The other three machines followed, and flew eastward, climbing, and taking up their battle stations. These attained, all five machines, taking their lead from Biggles, settled down to steady cruising speed. The desert, Ginger noticed, was much the same as that on the western side of the oasis.

It was nearly half an hour before the Whitley came into view, but once seen, the distance between it and its escort closed swiftly. It took no notice of the five machines above it, but held steadily on its course. Biggles swung round in a wide semi-circle, throttled back to the same speed as the decoy, and the trap was ready to spring.

For a long time nothing happened. The oasis came into view some distance to the south, but still the six machines went on, and on, until Ginger began to fear that the scheme had failed. Surely, if the Messerschmitts were coming they would have appeared by now? Suddenly the rocky country appeared ahead, and his nerves tingled, for it told him they were off their true course; the magnetic interference had been switched on, which suggested, if it did not actually prove, that the enemy was aware of the approach of a British aircraft.

Biggles knew the direction from which trouble would come, if it came, and his eyes focused themselves on the sun-tortured atmosphere that quivered above the rocky hills to the north-west; and watching, his eyes lit up in a smile of satisfaction as they found what they sought. Three specks were racing towards the Whitley, looking, from his superior altitude, like three winged insects crawling swiftly over the sand. Concentrating his attention on them he made them out to be Messerschmitt 109's. They were flying lower than he expected, which suggested, as he had predicted, that they were supremely confident, and had no doubt as to the result of the encounter with the big British machine. Biggles watched them, doing no more for the moment than alter his course slightly to put his machine—and at the same time those of his followers—in line with the sun. He waited until the Messerschmitts were about a mile away, and then, after a hand signal to Ginger and Tug, flying wing tip to wing tip on either side of him, he pushed his control column forward, and with his eyes on the leading Messerschmitt roared down in an almost vertical dive.

At this juncture an unexpected development brought a frown of anxiety to his forehead. The three Messerschmitts parted company, giving Biggles the impression that only one was going to attack while the other two would act as shepherds to prevent their apparently easy prey from escaping. What upset Biggles was the leading Messerschmitt's obvious intention of launching its attack from immediately below the Whitley. It was tearing down in a steep dive, obviously gathering speed for a vertical zoom, and it seemed as if this might happen before Biggles could get within effective range.

And this, in fact, did happen, although the attack did not end as Biggles feared it might, and as the Messerschmitt pilot evidentally thought it would. The Whitley, which had been cruising along as unconcernedly as a seagull, suddenly skidded round on its axis, and then banked sharply. A split second later a cloud of tracer* bullets burst from three places in the Whitley, converging on the Messerschmitt which, after

* Phosphorus loaded bullets whose course through the air can be seen by day or night.

a convulsive jerk at this unexpected reception, tore out of the field of fire like a scalded cat. Biggles' face broke into one of its rare grins of delight at this unexpected performance on the part of Bertie, whom he could imagine sitting at the controls of the Whitley with an irate, monocled eye, on his attacker.

Biggles' smile soon faded, however. The matter was too serious. The other Messerschmitts had also seen what had happened, for they had turned smartly towards the Whitley with the clear intention of attacking it on two sides. It was impossible for Biggles to watch all four machines, so leaving Ginger and Tug to deal with the two outside Messerschmitts he went straight at the leader who, having recovered somewhat from his fright, was returning to the attack with a greater exercise of caution. Pursuing the Whitley it is doubtful if he thought to look behind him; indeed, he could not have done so, or he would have been bound to see Biggles; and had he seen him he would have taken evasive action. As it was, he offered a perfect target, and as there are no rules in air combat, Biggles did not hesitate to take advantage of it.

Closing in to within a hundred feet to make sure there could be no mistake, he took the Messerschmitt in the red-crossed lines of his sight, and fired. It was only a short burst, but it was enough. It is doubtful if the Nazi pilot knew what had hit him. Pieces flew off his machine; it fell over on one wing, and slipped into a spin; one wing broke off at the roots, and the fuselage, spinning vertically round its remaining wing, its engine racing, plunged like a torpedo into the sand. Biggles knew that the pilot must have been killed by his burst of fire, or he would have baled out, or, at any rate, switched off his engine.

All this had happened in less time than it takes to tell. Even while his opponent was spinning Biggles had snatched a glance at the sky around him, for in modern air combat every second is vital. The scene had entirely changed. A second Messerschmitt, trailing behind it a sheet of white flame, was plunging earthward. Ginger and Tug were turning away from it, which told Biggles that they had both attacked the same machine, which was a mistake, for it left the third machine a chance to retreat, a chance it had not hesitated to take. Nose down, it was racing towards the north-west.

Again Biggles smiled grimly as he saw the Whitley in futile pursuit; as well might a frog have tried to catch a greyhound. Biggles, too, turned instinctively to follow the escaping machine, although he was doubtful if he would be able to overtake it—not that it really mattered, for looking up he saw Algy and Tex coming down like a pair of winged bombs to cut it off. Having the advantage of many thousands of feet of height, they would have no difficulty in doing this. The plan was working smoothly.

The end was rather unexpected. The pilot of the last Messerschmitt, who gave Biggles the impression of being new to the business, seemed to lose his head when he saw the two Spitfires appear out of the blue in front of him. He turned in a flash, to find himself faced with three more, for Ginger and Tug had joined in the pursuit. For a moment he wavered in indecision—and to waver in air combat is usually fatal. Algy got in a quick burst from long range—too long, Biggles thought, to be effective. The target may, or may not, have been hit; even Algy could not afterwards say for certain; but the pilot had had enough. He baled out. For three seconds he dropped like a stone, then his parachute blossomed out. The Messerschmitt, its dive steepening, struck the ground with terrific force, flinging a cloud of sand high into the air. Its pilot landed lightly not far away, relieved himself of his harness, and then stood staring up at those responsible for his misfortune.

Biggles circled over him wondering what to do. The plan had worked perfectly; all the enemy aircraft were down, but a factor had arisen for which he had not made provision. Now that the battle was over he put his profession as a pilot before nationality—a not uncommon thing with airmen—and the idea of leaving his defeated enemy to perish of thirst in the desert filled him with a repugnance that was not to be tolerated. There was, he realized, a chance that the enemy camp might send out a rescue party; this, however, did not mean that it would necessarily find the stranded Nazi pilot; and even if he were found he would, naturally, tell von Zoyton what had happened, and this Biggles was anxious to prevent.

He considered the situation with a worried frown, while the Whitley, and the other Spitfires, circled with him, waiting for a lead. The Nazi was still standing on the ground, looking up. Biggles could, at a pinch, have landed, and picked up the German; but the Whitley was obviously better fitted for the job if he could make Bertie understand what was required.

With this object in view he first flew very low over the area of sand on which the German was standing. As far as he could judge it was firm enough. He then flew close to the Whitley, close enough to see the pilot's face distinctly. Bertie, monocle in eye, made a face at him. Biggles perceived that something had upset him, but he couldn't be bothered to work out what it was.

Instead, he made a series of signals with his hand, jabbing his thumb down vigorously, which he hoped would be correctly interpreted. Bertie put his tongue out, presumably to indicate displeasure, but all the same he went down, and, to Biggles' relief, made a safe landing.

As the German—evidently understanding what was required—walked over to the big machine, Biggles found himself wondering what would have happened had the position been reversed.

The Whitley was only on the ground for about two minutes. As soon as the German was aboard it took off again. Satisfied that all was well, Biggles took a last glance at the other two Messerschmitts, lying where they had crashed. The pilots, he knew, were beyond all earthly help, so with the other machines behind him he led the way back to the oasis, disregarding his compass, relying on landmarks which his trained eye had noted on the outward journey.

The Whitley was the last to land, for as soon as the oasis came into view the five Spitfires went on, with the result that they were already parked when the Whitley taxied in, to unload before an astonished Biggles, not only Bertie and the German, but Taffy Hughes, Henry Harcourt and Ferocity Ferris. The three last-named jumped down laughing immoderately, but Bertie's face was flushed with indignation. The eye behind his monocle glinted as he marched straight up to Biggles.

'I object, sir,' he cried. 'Yes, absolutely. You can't do that sort of thing; no, by Jove—'

'What sort of thing?' asked Biggles, calmly.

'The way you snaffled my Hun! I call that a bit

thick—absolutely solid, in fact. He was my meat, absolutely, yes by Jingo—'

'You were jolly nearly his meat,' Biggles pointed out, coldly.

'Oh here, I say, did you hear that, chaps? I call that a bit hot—red hot, in fact. Me—his meat. Why, I had the blighter absolutely taped; all sewn up—'

'For the love of Mike,' broke in Biggles. 'What does it matter as long as we got him?'

Bertie looked shocked. 'I never thought to hear you say a think like that to a pal—no, by Jove,' he said, sadly. 'Wasn't it bad enough to have to fly your beastly old pantechnicon, without being pushed out of the scrum—if you see what I mean? You didn't give me a chance, no, not a bally look-in. I say that was a bit steep, absolutely sheer in fact—eh, you chaps?' Bertie turned to the grinning pilots for support.

'Never mind, Bertie, you did a good job,' said Biggles, consolingly. 'One day I'll find you a nice little Hun to play with all to yourself. Go and dip your head in a bucket of cold water—you'll feel better. What was the idea of taking the whole Karga contingent for a joyride? I didn't say that.'

Bertie shrugged his shoulders helplessly. 'That's what I told them,' he said pathetically. 'They got in and they wouldn't get out. They wouldn't take any notice of me, no jolly fear. Had the nerve to tell me to take a running jump at a bunch of dates.'

'Angus shouldn't have allowed it.'

'That's just what I told him,' declared Bertie, emphatically. 'And do you know what he said? He said they could come to man the guns in case there was a frolic before you turned up. The trip would give them a chance to see the jolly old desert, and all that sort of thing, and so on and so forth—if you see what I mean?'

'Yes, I see what you mean,' replied Biggles, keeping a straight face with difficulty. 'Well, I hope they enjoyed the scenery. As soon as we've had some lunch they can have the pleasure of taking the Whitley back to Karga. You'll have to go with them to get your Spitfire.'

Biggles turned to the prisoner, who had stood watching these proceedings with a sneer of contempt. He was young, in the early twenties, with flaxen hair and blue eyes, and might have been called good-looking had it not been for a surly expression and a truculent manner so pronounced that it was clearly cultivated rather than natural.

'Do you speak English?' inquired Biggles, in a friendly tone of voice.

The Nazi's right hand flew up. 'Heil Hitler!' he snapped.

Biggles nodded. 'Yes, we know all about that,' he said quietly. 'Try forgetting it for a little while.'

The German drew himself up stiffly. 'I understand I am a prisoner,' he said in fairly good English.

'That's something, at any rate,' murmured Ginger.

Biggles ignored the German's rudeness. 'I invite you to give me your parole while you are here; we would rather treat you as a guest than a prisoner.'

'I prefer to be a prisoner,' was the haughty reply.

'How about trying to be a gentleman for a change?' suggested Henry Harcourt.

'I'd knock his perishing block off,' growled Tug Carrington.

'Will you fellows please leave the talking to me?' said Biggles, coldly. Then, to the prisoner, 'Years ago, officers in the air services—and that includes your fellows as well as ours—when we weren't fighting, managed to forget our quarrels. It made things more pleasant. I'm not asking for an indefinite parole—merely for while you are here with us.'

'Things are different now,' returned the German, with a sneer.

'Yes, so it seems,' replied Biggles, a trifle sadly.

'I shall escape,' said the German loudly.

'Quite right. I should do the same thing were I in your position, but I wouldn't shout about it. There are ways of doing these things, you know—or perhaps you don't know. What's your name?'

'Find out!'

Biggles' face hardened, and he took a pace nearer. 'Listen here,' he said. 'I'm not asking you to tell me anything to which I am not entitled under the Rules of War*. I'm trying to be patient with you. Now, what is your name?'

The German hesitated. Perhaps there was something in Biggles' quiet manner that made him think twice. 'Heinrich Hymann,' he said, grudgingly.

'Rank?'

'*Leutnant***.'

'Thank you. Let's go in and have some lunch.'

---

* Under international agreement a prisoner of war is only obliged to tell his name, rank and service number.

** German rank equivalent to Pilot officer.

Chapter 6
Biggles Strikes Again

After lunch, which the prisoner shared, sitting with the other officers, Biggles' considerate manner remained unaltered; and it was perhaps for this reason that the Nazi thawed somewhat—or it might be better to say, became reconciled. Several times he looked at Biggles strangely, as if he suspected that his courteous behaviour was but a pose to deceive him.

When the meal was over he stood up, turned to Biggles, bowed stiffly from the waist, and announced that he was prepared to give his parole not to attempt to escape while he was with the squadron.

'That's all right,' answered Biggles, evenly. 'I accept your parole, as long as you understand that a parole is a matter of honour, and therefore inviolate while it lasts. You can end it any time you like by giving me five minutes' notice.'

The German bowed again, smiling faintly. 'Am I at liberty to take some fresh air?'

'Certainly, but keep to this part of the oasis.' Biggles walked to the door with the prisoner to point out which part he meant.

Tex frowned. 'I wouldn't trust that guy as far as a rattlesnake can strike,' he told Tug in a quiet aside. 'In Texas we make sure of his sort—with a rope.'

'I wouldn't let the C.O.* hear you talking like that,'

* Commanding Officer.

interposed Ginger softly. 'If Biggles has a weakness, it is judging other people by his own principles, and I, for one, wouldn't have it any other way. It hasn't done us much harm so far. Anyway, I don't think even a Nazi would break his parole.'

'A Nazi would break anything,' grated Tex.

Bertie looked horrified. 'Oh, here, I say, old rustler, that's going a bit far—yes, by Jove, too bally far. I couldn't imagine even a double-dyed Nazi breaking his word of honour.'

'No, *you* couldn't,' put in Tug pointedly. 'I'd anchor him to a rock with a couple of cables—that's how he'd have treated any of us.' He looked up to see Biggles' eyes on him.

'Are you suggesting,' inquired Biggles icily, 'that we arrange our code of behaviour by what a Nazi would do?'

'Er—no, sir.'

'Good. I thought for a moment you were. I hate moralizing, but it's my experience that liars sooner or later run into something sticky—and that goes for Hymann. He's an officer, and until he turns out to be something else I shall treat him as one. He can be flown up to Egypt as soon as I can spare the Whitley. Let it go at that. Get your combat reports made out and we'll talk things over.'

On the whole Biggles was well satisfied with the progress he had made, but was in some doubt as to his next step. In accordance with his usual custom he discussed it with the others, to give them an opportunity of expressing their opinions.

'The obvious course would be to fly over and make a reconnaissance, to try to locate the Boche aerodrome,' he admitted in reply to a question by Ginger. 'You

71

might say, let's find their nest now we know roughly where it is, and bomb them out of the Libyan desert. On the face of it there is much to recommend the plan, but I'm not convinced that it is the right one—at any rate not yet. The success of such a plan would depend on absolute success, and that's something we can't guarantee. Suppose we failed to find the German landing-ground, and they saw us—and they certainly would see us—it would be us who got the bombs. In any case, if it came to a general clash there would be casualties on our side as well as theirs; and while I don't expect to fight a war without getting hurt, if casualties can be avoided, provided we achieve our object, so much the better. The Nazis have got where they have in this war by employing unorthodox methods. Well, two can play at that game. We played the first trick this morning, and it came off. Not only has the enemy lost three machines without loss to ourselves, but—and this is important—he doesn't know what caused his casualties. That will worry him.'

'What you really mean is,' put in Algy smoothly, 'you've got another trick up your sleeve? Let's hear it.'

Biggles smiled. 'Quite right,' he confessed. 'It's rather more risky than the one we played this morning, but it struck me that we might give the Whitley another airing before we sent it back to Karga.'

Bertie was industriously polishing his eyeglass. 'I hope, sir, that on this occasion you'll trundle the jolly old steam-roller through the atmosphere—if you get my meaning,' he remarked.

'That was my intention. This is the scheme. I propose, first of all, to broadcast a radio signal that a British aircraft, G-UROK, is leaving Karga forthwith.'

Algy wrinkled his forehead. 'But the enemy will pick the message up.'

'Of course—that's why I'm sending it out.'

'But they must have picked up the same message early this morning?'

'Quite right. They won't know what to make of it, particularly as three of their machines went out to intercept the aircraft and did not return. They won't be able to solve the mystery sitting at home, so what will they do? Unless I've missed my mark, von Zoyton and his boys will beetle along to see what the deuce is really happening.'

'They'll catch you in the Whitley.'

'Exactly.'

'With an escort?'

'No, there will be no escort.'

'Are you crazy?'

'I hope not. As soon as I see the swastikas coming I shall lose my nerve, go down and land, choosing a nice open space if there is one handy.'

'Go on,' invited Algy. 'What happens next?'

'Von Zoyton and his crowd, seeing the machine go down, will land to examine the prize. When they reach the Whitley they will find us waiting to receive them.'

'Us? Who do you mean?'

'Well, several of us—say, half a dozen, with Tommy guns*. The principle is the same as that played by the Navy with their Q-ships. You remember how it works? A harmless-looking craft is sent out inviting trouble, but when it is attacked it turns out to be a red-hot tartar, bristling with guns. Someone will have to stay

---

* A sub-machine gun, the original designed by Thompson.

73

here to take charge, and form a reserve in case the plan comes unstuck.'

There were smiles as Biggles divulged his plan.

'Suppose von Zoyton, or whoever attacks the Whitley, doesn't land?' asked Ginger.

'If they don't land, obviously they will return to their base and report the position of the aircraft, when, if the same procedure as before is followed, a car will be sent out to collect the stranded passengers. We shall be there, waiting, so it will come to the same thing in the end. We ought to be able to gather some more prisoners, and perhaps a car.'

'And what next, sir?' asked Henry Harcourt.

'I think that's enough to go on with,' answered Biggles. 'Our next move will depend on how things pan out. There are all sorts of possibilities.'

'When are you going to start this operation?' asked Algy.

Biggles glanced at his watch and considered the question for a moment before he replied.

'Just when you fellows feel like it. You've done one show to-day. If you feel that the heat is trying we'll leave it until to-morrow. There's no desperate hurry; on the other hand, if you feel up to it, there is no reason why we shouldn't do the show this afternoon. We're not out here on a picnic. Our job is to make the route safe, and the sooner it is safe, the better.'

There was a chorus of voices in favour of doing the show that day. Bertie voiced the view that it was better to do something than do nothing, because there was less time to think about the heat.

'All right,' agreed Biggles. 'Consider it settled. I shan't need everybody. Six people in the Whitley, with a couple of Tommy guns, and revolvers, ought to be a match for anything that turns up. I shall fly the Whitley. The other five will be chosen by drawing lots—that's the fairest way. Algy, you'll have to stay here to take charge. You'd better send someone to Karga to let Angus know that we're all right, and that the Whitley will be returning shortly—possibly to-night. Now put all the names except yours and mine in a hat.'

This was soon done, with the result that the operating party turned out to be: Biggles, in command; Lord Bertie, Tex, Tug, Taffy Hughes and Ferocity Ferris. This left Algy, Ginger, and Henry Harcourt to remain at the oasis. They looked glum, but said nothing.

Algy went off to the radio tent to arrange for the despatch of the fake signal announcing the departure of the commercial aircraft. The others went to the armoury where weapons were drawn and tested, and the party inspected by Biggles, who allowed some time to elapse before he climbed into the cockpit of the Whitley. It was, therefore, well on in the afternoon when the big machine, with the operating party on board, took off and cruised towards the west.

Crossing the caravan road, Biggles turned to the north, towards the area where he had found Ginger, which, as he now knew, was the direction of the enemy camp. Ignoring his compass, which he dare no longer trust, he flew entirely by landmarks noted on his previous flights. Apart from the brief occasions when he checked up on these, his attention was directed entirely to the sky around him. He knew he was doing a risky thing, and had no intention of being caught unaware. The lives of everyone on board might well depend on his spotting the enemy aircraft before they came within range, and getting on the ground before they could open fire. Bertie sat beside him and shared his task. Taffy occupied the forward gun turret, and Tug, the rear, so they were really in a position to put up a fight if they were caught in the air by a force of fighters; but that was not Biggles' intention if it could be avoided; apart from anything else, it involved risks which he preferred not to take.

As it turned out, there was no air battle. Biggles saw three specks appear in the sky in the direction from which he expected the enemy to come. Evidently they saw no reason to employ stalking tactics, for they made straight for the Whitley.

'Here they come,' said Biggles calmly. 'Hang on, Bertie, I may have to move smartly.'

Now Biggles did not want to arouse suspicion by giving in too easily; on the other hand, he had no wish to offer himself as a target; so he chose a middle course. As the three Messerschmitts drew close he started skidding wildly about the sky, employing exaggerated evading tactics to create an impression that he was in a panic. One of the enemy machines took a long shot at him with his cannon, and that was really all Biggles was waiting for. He had already chosen his emergency landing ground—as before, a strip of sand between two outcrops of rock—and as the tracer shells screamed over him he cut his engine and side-slipped steeply towards it. In two minutes he was on the ground, deliberately finishing his run within a few yards of the rock boundary.

'Don't show yourselves, but be ready to get out in a hurry,' he shouted.

It was a strange moment, brittle with expectation, yet to those in the aircraft, unsatisfactory, for there was

76

nothing they could do. Biggles' sensation was chiefly one of anxiety, for he did not like the way the Messerschmitts were behaving. All three had reached the Whitley within a minute of its landing; two had remained comparatively high, at perhaps a thousand feet, circling; the other, apparently the leader, which sported a blue airscrew boss and fin, had dived low in a manner which, as the slim fuselage flashed over his head, gave Biggles the impression that the pilot was aiming his guns at the Whitley, and would have fired had he not overshot his mark. It was a contingency for which Biggles had not made allowances, and his anxiety rose swiftly to real alarm as the Messerschmitt swung round in a business-like way, clearly with the intention of repeating the dive. There appeared to be no reason for such a manœuvre unless the pilot intended to carry out offensive action against the helpless Whitley.

Suddenly Biggles shouted, 'Get outside, everybody. Take your guns and find cover amongst the rocks. Jump to it!'

Knowing that the order would be obeyed, he did not wait to watch the performance of it, but made a hurried exit from the aircraft and took cover behind an outcrop of rock some twenty yards away. The others had selected similar positions near at hand. They were only just in time, for within a few seconds the blue-nosed Messerschmitt was diving steeply on the aircraft, raking it with both machine-gun and cannon fire. It was a nasty moment, for bullets and shells not only smashed through the machine, but zipped viciously into the sand and thudded against the rocks behind which the British pilots lay. There were some narrow escapes, but no one was hit.

Again the Messerschmitt pilot roared round, and

diving, lashed the Whitley with a hail of fire as though it had done him a personal injury; and this time he was even more successful, for a tongue of flame from the riddled fuselage had licked hungrily along the fabric. In a minute the entire machine was a blazing inferno.

Biggles said nothing. There was nothing to say. This time the enemy had not behaved quite as he expected, and the result was a blow that might well prove fatal. The Messerschmitt that had done the damage, apparently satisfied with its work, now came low, circling in a flat turn to watch the conflagration, while his two companions, acting either under orders or on their own initiative, turned away and disappeared towards the north-west.

Bertie polished his eyeglass imperturbably. 'Nasty fellow,' he observed. 'It's going to be beastly hot walking home, what?'

But Biggles wasn't listening. With an expression of incredulity on his face he was watching a new arrival that now came racing on full throttle towards the scene. There was no need to look twice to recognize the type. It was a Spitfire. There were cries and ejaculations from the earthbound airmen.

When Biggles spoke his voice was pitched high with astonishment. 'Why, that's Ginger's machine!' he exclaimed. 'What the dickens does the young fool think he's doing . . . ?' Biggles' voice trailed away to silence, as drama, swift and vicious, developed.

The Spitfire was flying unswervingly, flat out on a north-westerly course. From its behaviour it might have been pursuing the two departing Messerschmitts. The pilot, whose eyes were probably on the two German machines which, while distant, were still in sight, appeared not to see the blue-nosed Messerschmitt now zooming upward in a beautiful climbing turn into the eye of the sun. For a moment it hung there, like a hawk about to strike; then it turned on its wing and descended on the Spitfire like a bolt from the blue. As it came into range its guns flashed, and tracer bullets made a glittering line between the two machines.

The result was never in doubt. The stricken Spitfire jerked up on its tail, shedding fabric and metal, its airscrew making a gleaming arc of light as it threshed vainly at the air; then, with a slow deliberation that was more ghastly to watch than speed, it rolled over on its back; the nose swung down, and with a crescendo wail of agony it dropped like a stone to strike the gleaming sand not a hundred yards from where Biggles, tense and ashen-faced, stood watching. There was a roaring, splintering crash. A sheet of white flame leapt skywards. Black oily smoke rolled up behind it.

Came silence, a brittle attentive silence broken only by the brisk crackle of the burning aircraft, and the drone of the machine that had destroyed it. Biggles, stunned for once into immobility, still stood and stared, paralyzed by the suddenness of the tragedy. Then he turned to where the others lay, pale and saucer-eyed. 'Stay where you are,' he said in a curiously calm voice. 'We can't do anything.'

He himself, although he knew that anything he did would be futile, ran towards the blazing mass of wreckage, holding up his arms as he drew near to shield his face from the fierce heat. Twenty yards was as near as he could get. Apart from the heat, cartridges were exploding, flinging bullets in all directions. Knowing that whoever was in the machine must be already burnt to a cinder, he walked slowly back to where the Whitley

79

had nearly burnt itself out and sank down on a boulder. 'Stay under cover,' he told the others in a dead voice.

The blue-nosed Messerschmitt was still circling, losing height, but he took little notice of it. He bore the pilot no particular malice. What he had done was no more than Biggles would have done had the position been reversed. Professionally, the shooting down of the Spitfire had been a brilliant piece of work, precisely timed and perfectly executed. Biggles sat still, trying to think. Nothing now could restore the Spitfire pilot to life, but he found it impossible not to wonder what had brought it there.

Bertie interrupted his melancholy reverie. 'That fellow's going to land,' he said.

Looking up, Biggles saw that it was true. The Messerschmitt pilot had cut his engine, lowered his wheels, and was sideslipping into the gully in which the Whitley had come down, with the obvious intention of landing.

Biggles smiled wanly at the others. 'This is what I'd hope he'd do,' he murmured. 'Unfortunately, he did a few other things first. Stay where you are, all of you.'

The Messerschmitt pilot landed near the burning Spitfire. He jumped down, and after a casual glance at it walked on towards the spot where Biggles still sat on his rock, smoking a cigarette. As he drew near Biggles made him out to be a man of about twenty-five, tall, agile, and virile, but with that hardness of expression common to the fanatical Nazi. With a revolver consciously displayed in his hand he walked straight up to Biggles, who did not move.

'You are my prisoner,' he announced, with the usual Nazi arrogance that never failed to fill Biggles with wonder. He spoke in English, with a strong accent.

Biggles was in no mood to argue. 'Put that gun away, shut up and sit down,' he said coldly. 'This time you've captured more than you bargained for.' He turned to the others. 'All right, you chaps, you can come out now,' he said wearily.

Had the circumstances been different he might have smiled at the expression on the Nazi's face when five R.A.F. officers stood up and came from the rocks behind which they had lain concealed.

'What—what is this—a trick?' rasped the Nazi furiously.

'Just a reception committee,' answered Biggles. 'My name, by the way, is Bigglesworth. What's yours?'

The other clicked his heels. 'Hauptmann Rudolf von Zoyton.'

Biggles nodded. 'I won't say I'm glad to meet you,' he said evenly. 'You people are beginning to get my goat. It wouldn't take much to make me angry, so you'd better keep your mouth shut.' Turning to Tex, he added, 'Take his gun and keep an eye on him. If he tries any rough stuff you have my permission to punch him on the nose.' Then, to Bertie, 'Come over here, I want to speak to you.'

Taking Bertie out of earshot of the German he went on, 'I'm afraid this is a bad show. We're in a jam. Without the Whitley we've no transport back to the oasis, unless the Germans send their car out to us. If they do we shall have to grab it. It's our only chance of getting away. We can last the night without water, and possible until noon to-morrow, but no longer. Fortunately, we have one way of getting into touch with Algy—the Messerschmitt. I'm going to fly it home and fetch a few cans of water, but before doing that, as we are so close, I'm going to have a dekko at the Nazi aerodrome. You can take care of things here until I get back. See you later.' Biggles strode away towards the blue-nosed enemy aircraft.

Chapter 7
Events at the Oasis

When Biggles had left the oasis in the Whitley, Algy,
Ginger and Henry Harcourt had watched the machine
out of sight before returning to the shade of the palms.
There was only one duty to be done, and that was, as
Biggles had ordered, to notify Angus, at Karga, that
his absent officers were all right and would be returning
shortly. That meant, of course, that someone would
have to fly to Karga in a Spitfire, and as Algy, being
in charge at the oasis, could not leave it, the matter
resolved itself into a choice between Ginger and Henry.
Algy didn't care who went as long as the message was
taken, and left it to the two officers to decide between
themselves who should go.

Both wanted to go, possibly because loafing about
the oasis with nothing to do was a depressing form of
boredom. Clearly, there was only one fair way of settling the issue, and that was to toss for it. Ginger, to
his disgust, lost the toss, and Henry, with a whoop of
triumph, departed in the direction of the aircraft park.

'Can I use your machine?' he shouted over his
shoulder as he walked away. 'Mine's at Karga.'

'All right,' agreed Ginger, 'but if you break it I'll
break your neck.' He strolled on to find Algy, and
found him lying in the shade of a palm, apparently in
earnest contemplation of the intricate tracery of fronds
overhead.

'Make yourself comfortable,' invited Algy.

Ginger sat down beside him. 'Henry is pushing off to Karga right away.'

Algy grunted. He wasn't particularly interested.

'Where's Hymann?' asked Ginger.

'I left him sitting near the spring,' answered Algy. 'I tipped off the flight sergeant to keep an eye on him. He's a surly brute—I don't want him here with me.'

The restful silence was suddenly shattered by the starting growl of an aero engine.

'That must be Henry,' murmured Ginger. 'I'll go and see him off, and then come back.' He got up and walked away through the palms in the direction of the sound.

It happened that between him and the machines there was an open, sandy glade, and for this reason he had a clear view of what was going on. It was as he expected. A mechanic was in the cockpit of his Spitfire having just started up the engine for Henry, who was adjusting his dark glasses and sun helmet preparatory to taking over from the mechanic. Flight-Sergeant Smyth and a number of airmen were working at a test bench not far away. Sitting under a tree near them, as Algy had described, was Hymann, who now rose to his feet and strolled, hands in pockets, towards the Spitfire, not unnaturally, to watch it take off. He was a good deal nearer than Ginger, and consequently reached the machine first. There was nothing in his manner to arouse suspicion, and, in fact, probably because the German was on parole, no suspicion of anything wrong entered Ginger's mind.

What happened next occurred with the speed of light. The mechanic, having finished his task, climbed out of the cockpit on to the wing, and jumped lightly to the ground. At the same time Henry stepped forward to take his place, and had lifted one foot to the wing, when Hymann, with a tigerish leap, sprang forward, swinging a heavy spanner in his hand. It descended on the head of the mechanic, whose back was turned, and who, therefore, did not see the blow struck. Ginger did, and with a warning shout dashed forward. The shout was lost in the mutter of the engine, but something made Henry turn. He was just in time to see the mechanic sink unconscious to the ground. He also saw who was responsible, and what he did was perfectly natural. He jumped off the wing to grapple with the Nazi who, without pausing for an instant, had jumped over the prone body of the mechanic with a view to striking down Henry, and so reaching the cockpit.

Ginger saw all this as he raced towards the scene, but he was not in time to help Henry, who was not only unarmed, but a good deal lighter than the German. There was a brief struggle, and then the spanner came down on Henry's head with a force that would certainly have split his skull had not the sun helmet taken some of the shock of the blow. Henry staggered away, reeling drunkenly, and fell. Moving with feline speed the Nazi sprang into the cockpit and opened the throttle wide. The Spitfire jumped forward, head-on towards Ginger, who was still some ten yards or so away. He had to leap aside to avoid the whirling airscrew, but made a grab at the leading edge of the port wing. But the machine was now moving fast; the wing struck him across the chest; for a moment he clung to it desperately, but there was nothing for his clawing fingers to grasp. They slipped off the polished surface and he went down heavily on his back. The aircraft raced on, and reached the aisle that gave access to the open sand.

Mouthing with rage Ginger dashed after it, although he knew that nothing now, except a gun, could prevent the aircraft from getting away. The flight sergeant and several mechanics also ran after it, although they were just as helpless. Ginger threw up his arms in impotent fury as the Spitfire reached the sand and shot like an arrow into the air.

'Start up another machine!' yelled Ginger to the flight sergeant. He was dancing in his rage.

Algy came running up. 'What's going on?' he demanded.

'Hymann's got away. The swine brained one of the mechanics. Henry is hurt, too. Look after them. I'm going after Hymann. I'll get that skunk if I have to follow him to Timbuctoo.'

But a Spitfire is not started in a second, and it was nearly five minutes before Ginger, in Henry's machine, was lined up ready to take off. Ginger fumed at the delay. The instant the machine was ready he scrambled into the cockpit and taxied tail-up to the take-off ground, and so into the air. Hymann was already out of sight, but he knew the direction he had taken and settled down to follow.

His boiling rage cooled to a calculating simmer of anger, and he began to think more clearly. The desire for revenge against the perfidious Nazi became secondary to the necessity for putting him out of action, if it were possible, before he could report the presence of Biggles' squadron at Salima Oasis to his chief. If the Nazi got away, and Ginger was afraid he might, Biggles' present plan might be completely upset.

Ginger flew flat out with his eyes on the sky, hoping to catch sight of his now hated foe. He could not forget or forgive the foul blow that had struck down the unsuspecting mechanic. Moreover, that the Nazi should escape was bad enough, but that he should take his, Ginger's, Spitfire with him, added insult to injury.

The others had been right, thought Ginger moodily, as he roared on. Biggles should not have accepted a Nazi's parole. It was clear now that Hymann had only given it in order to obtain the freedom that made escape possible. So brooded Ginger in his anger as he sped on with his eyes questing the sky. Only occasionally did he glance at the ground to check up on his course.

He was not to know that even if the machine he was flying was capable of doubling its speed he would never overhaul the Nazi, for the simple reason that the German lay in a tangle of charred wreckage among the rocks, shot down, by a stroke of ironic justice, by his own commanding officer, von Zoyton. He had already passed it, and the burnt-out Whitley, without seeing either; and if it appears strange that he did not see these grim remains, it must be remembered that his eyes were on the sky, not the ground; and, moreover, he was flying low, for he had not wasted precious seconds climbing for height. His brain was racing in a single track—the thought of Hymann, and what his escape might mean; and for that reason he did not consider the risks he was taking in approaching enemy territory, risks which, in the ordinary way, might have given him reason to pause in his headlong pursuit.

He had already reached a point farther to the north-west than he had ever been before, but because he was low he was able to make out two landmarks which, by a curious chance, he had seen from a distance. These were the two rock formations which he had observed when lying on the ground with Biggles on the occasion when they had watched the searchlight. One was the mass of rock shaped like a frog, and the other, the four spires.

Still seeking his quarry he raced on over the first. A few minutes later he roared over the second, and as he did so he saw something that brought a flush of exultation to his cheeks. Away ahead he picked out a speck in the sky, circling over what he presently made out to be an oasis not unlike Salima. At first, probably because his mind was centred on it, he thought the aircraft was a Spitfire, and it was not until he drew close that he saw, with a pang of disappointment, that he had been mistaken. The machine was a Messerschmitt 109, with a blue nose and fin. Ginger's mouth set in a thin line. He was in the mood for a fight, and he was prepared to fight anything. Hymann, apparently, had got away, but the Messerschmitt would at least provide him with a satisfying target. With great consideration, he thought, it had turned towards him — or at any rate, it was now coming in his direction. Holding the joystick forward for a moment for maximum speed he pulled up in a rocket zoom that took him up behind the Messerschmitt. The instant he was level with it he pulled the Spitfire on its back, and then half rolled to even keel. In a split second he had fired his first burst. But in some mysterious way the Messerschmitt had flicked into a vertical bank and so avoided his fire. It seemed that the Messerschmitt preferred to take evading action rather than fight, for it now did its best to avoid combat. Flinging his machine on its side he dragged the joystick back into his right thigh, which for a second brought his sights in line with the Messerschmitt's tail. Again his guns streamed flame, spitting lines of tracer bullets across the intervening distance. This time they hit their mark, but even in that moment of speed and action Ginger found time to wonder why the Messerschmitt pilot made no attempt to return his fire, for there had been a brief opportunity for him to do so.

But that didn't matter now. The blue fin was shattered. An elevator broke off, and the machine reeled before going into the spin from which it could never recover. Ginger was not surprised to see the pilot fling open the hood of his cockpit, climb out on to the wing and launch himself into space. His parachute opened, arresting his headlong fall, and he floated downwards.

Ginger watched the falling pilot for a moment; then his eyes looked past him at the ground. He was startled, but not surprised, to see four Messerschmitts racing across the sand in a frenzied take-off. This was more than he was prepared to take on single-handed, and prudence counselled retreat while there was time. He waited only for a moment to survey the ground for the missing Spitfire, but it was not there, which puzzled him, for he thought Hymann could barely have had time to put the machine out of sight. Turning, he headed for home. He had plenty of height, so he did not fear that the Messerschmitts would catch him. Nor did they. A few minutes later, when he looked back, he could see no sign of them.

Looking down at the ground, however, he saw something else, something that made him hold his breath in astonishment. Lying close to each other were two black airframes, obviously burnt-out aircraft. Near the larger one six figures stood waving. Six people? Why, he thought, that must be Biggles and the others. Strangely enough, in his excitement he had forgotten all about the Whitley. Now he remembered, and wondered what Biggles would have to say about his ill-advised behaviour. He decided to go down and get it over. In any case, Biggles ought to know about Hymann getting away. Choosing a suitable spot he glided down, and having landed, walked briskly to where the little group awaited him.

He noticed at once that Biggles was not there. He observed, too, the German officer. But what puzzled him most was the expression on the faces of his friends. With their eyes round with wonder they simply stood and stared at him. Bertie muttered incoherently, making meaningless signs with his hands.

'What's the matter with all of you?' demanded Ginger. 'Is there something odd about me?'

Bertie pointed at the burnt-out Spitfire. 'That's—that's—your machine, old boy. We thought you were flying the bally thing.'

Understanding burst upon Ginger. 'Great Scott!' he cried. 'How did it happen?'

Tug answered. He indicated von Zoyton with his thumb. 'He did it. Who was in the machine—Henry?'

'Why, no,' gasped Ginger. 'It was Hymann. He broke his parole and bolted in my Spit. So *that's* what happened to him. No wonder I couldn't overtake him. It seems as though Biggles was right, as usual. Hymann's lying didn't get him far. By the way, where is Biggles?'

'Gone to have a dekko at the German landing ground, look you,' replied Taffy.

Ginger stared. He pointed at the remains of the Whitley. 'I thought that was the Whitley!' he exclaimed.

'It was,' Bertie told him. 'Von Zoyton made a bonfire of it before he landed.'

'But—but you hadn't another machine?' cried Ginger. 'What did Biggles use?'

Tug grinned. 'He borrowed von Zoyton's kite for the evening.'

A ghastly thought struck Ginger, turning his blood cold and making his knees weak. His tongue flicked over his lips as though he had difficulty in speaking. 'It wasn't . . . it wasn't by any chance a Messerschmitt—with a blue nose?' he gulped.

'Sure, that's the bird,' declared Tex cheerfully. 'Say! What's wrong?'

Ginger clapped a hand to his forehead. 'Heaven help me,' he breathed in an awe-stricken whisper. 'I've just shot him down.'

There was dead silence for a moment. Then Bertie spoke. 'Where did it happen?'

Ginger swallowed. 'Right over the enemy aerodrome,' he answered chokingly. 'So that's why he didn't return my fire!'

Von Zoyton laughed harshly.

Chapter 8
A Desperate Venture

Ginger ignored the German. He was overcome by the
state of affairs that had arisen, and his paramount
sensation at that moment was one of utter helplessness.
Not only was Biggles a prisoner—for he could not
imagine that he had escaped capture—but the entire
squadron was threatened with extinction. One Spitfire
was the only connecting link with the base, and he
wondered vaguely whether it would be possible to
transport the others home one by one, or if he should
ask them to walk, while he dropped food and water to
them during their long journey to the oasis.

To make matters more difficult the sun was now low
over the horizon. In the desert, during the blinding
glare of day, nothing appears to change. The sun seems
to be always at the zenith, as though it could never
again sink below the earth. But when once it begins to
fall, it falls ever faster. The rocks, as though they had
been driven into the sand by the hammering rays, begin
to rise. Shadows appear, and behind the level beams
assume fantastic shapes, with an eerie effect on the
whole barren scene. Thus it was now. Soon, very soon,
night would fall.

Ginger took Bertie out of earshot of the German and
asked him what he intended to do, for in the absence
of Biggles, Bertie, by virtue of his rank of Flight
Lieutenant, automatically took command of the detach-
ment.

'It's dooced awkward,' muttered Bertie. 'If we go towards the enemy we shall all be captured. If we stay here we shall fry when the sun comes up to-morrow. To try to get home means abandoning the C.O. Yes, by Jove, it's awkward. Confounded nuisance having von Zoyton with us, too. I'm really no good at this sort of thing, you know.'

At this juncture an unexpected sound became audible. It was the purr of an internal combustion engine, some distance away.

'What on earth is that?' demanded Bertie.

Ginger guessed, and he guessed correctly. 'I'll bet it's the car—you know, the car the Germans send out to crashed machines.'

'By jingo! I'd clean forgotten all about it,' admitted Bertie. 'This is really most awfully nice of them—yes, by jove! I'd rather ride home than walk, every time. We'll take the car.'

'Keep an eye on von Zoyton,' said Ginger tersely. 'He knows what's coming, and may try to yell a warning.' So saying he scrambled to the top of the rock and looked out across the desert. He was back in a moment, looking agitated. 'It isn't going to be as easy as we thought,' he muttered. 'It's an *armoured* car.'

'Is it, though?' murmured Bertie, unperturbed, and then went on to make his dispositions. 'Tex, old boy, take von Zoyton out of sight. If he starts squealing, hit him on the boko. We can't have any half measures— no, absolutely. The rest of you chaps get under cover with your guns ready. This is going to be fine.'

While the order was being obeyed, Bertie sat on the boulder once occupied by Biggles, adjusted his monocle and waited.

Presently the car appeared, travelling slowly on

account of the uneven nature of the ground. A head and shoulders projected above the centre turret. Still it came on, obviously without the crew having the slightest suspicion that anything was wrong. There was, in fact, nothing to indicate to the driver or the crew that von Zoyton, as they would naturally suppose, was not in charge of the situation. On the contrary, the presence of the burnt Whitley was calculated to convey the opposite impression.

'Don't move, chaps, until I put up my hand—then make a rush,' Bertie told the others. 'We don't want any shooting if it can be avoided; it's too beastly hot.'

With the only sound the steady purr of its engine, the armoured vehicle, bristling with guns, ran up to where Bertie was sitting in a disconsolate attitude. The man in the gun turret called something to him, but he did not answer, for the words were German and he did not understand them. The head and shoulders disappeared. The side door was thrown open and three men emerged, casually wiping perspiration from their faces.

Bertie strolled over to the car and looked inside. One man, the driver, remained, lounging behind the wheel. He beckoned to him. The man, with an expression of wonder on his face, joined the others on the sand. All four stared at Bertie. It was obvious from their manner that they could not make out what was going on. They still apprehended no danger. Even when Bertie raised his hand and Ginger, Tug, Ferocity and Taffy emerged, Ginger and Taffy carrying Tommy guns, they merely looked stupefied. The guns must have told them that something was wrong, but they seemed unable to grasp what precisely had happened.

'Sorry, and all that, but you are prisoners,' said

Bertie apologetically, regarding them steadily through his monocle.

They understood that, for there was a mutter of conversation.

Inquiry produced the information that the party comprised a driver, a mechanic, a medical orderly, and the Italian officer Pallini, who had acted as guide.

Bertie put them with von Zoyton and, leaving Tex, Tug and Ferocity on guard, took Ginger and Taffy on one side.

'I say, you fellows, this is getting a bit thick,' he remarked. 'I'm dashed if I know what to do next. Are we going to stay here all night? It'll be dark in five minutes. I'm not much good at thinking things out— no good at all, in fact. Give me a bat and I can hit the jolly old ball, and all that sort of thing, but when it comes to arranging the teams I'm no bally use.'

'How many people could we get in the car?' asked Ginger.

Bertie didn't know, so Taffy went to look.

'Eight, or nine at a pinch,' he announced when he returned.

'Dear—dear,' murmured Bertie. 'How dashed awkward. There are eleven of us in the party already. I'm no bally sardine.'

'We can't go without Biggles, anyway,' Ginger pointed out. 'We must try to get hold of him somehow.'

'Yes, absolutely,' agreed Bertie. 'But how?'

'Biggles always seems able to work these things out,' said Ginger. 'There must be a way, if only we can think of it.'

The fact of the matter was, they were beginning to miss Biggles.

'Give me a few minutes to think,' suggested Ginger.

'I may be able to work out a plan. This bunch of prisoners is going to take a bit of handling, so I suggest for a start that we send for reinforcements. Algy ought to know what has happened, anyway. He could get out here, so could Henry if he wasn't badly hurt. That would give us two more machines. I'd send Ferocity home in my Spitfire to tell Algy what has happened. While that's going on some of us could take the car and try to rescue Biggles.'

'How shall we find the enemy camp?' asked Taffy.

'By following the wheel tracks—that ought to be easy. Let me think this over.'

Ten minutes later he gave an outline of his plan. Ferocity had already taken off in the Spitfire to report to Algy. That left five officers available for duty. Two would be needed to guard the five prisoners, who might be expected to make a dash for liberty in the darkness should an opportunity present itself. That left three available for the rescue party. This, Ginger suggested, should consist of himself, Bertie and Taffy. The idea was that they should follow the wheel marks to some point near the enemy camp, which, he thought, was not more than twenty to thirty miles away. There, assuming that the presence of the car was not detected, one could remain at the wheel of the vehicle while the other two went forward to reconnoitre, and, if possible, locate Biggles. Their actions would then depend on what they found. Without knowing the dispositions of the enemy aerodrome it was impossible to plan any further.

'I say, old boy, that doesn't sound much of a plan to me,' protested Bertie.

'What's wrong with it?'

'Well, there isn't any plan at all. It's too simple—if you get what I mean.'

'The simplicity is probably the best thing about it,' declared Ginger. 'The more involved the scheme the easier it is to go wrong. I've heard Biggles say that a score of times. If we stand here talking we shan't get anywhere. If we're going to try to get Biggles, the sooner we start moving the better, otherwise we shall arrive there in time to discover that he's on his way to Germany.'

'Too true, too true,' murmured Bertie. 'Let's go. Who's going to drive the chariot?'

'I'll drive, look you,' offered Taffy. 'I once drove a tank.'

'I know all about that,' returned Ginger grimly. 'I also know why they used to call you "Crasher." Be careful how you handle this char-a-banc, because if you bust it we shan't get another.'

Taffy promised to be careful, so leaving Tex and Tug in charge of the prisoners, Bertie, Taffy and Ginger went over to the car, taking one of the Tommy guns with them. They also carried revolvers. Finding a petrol can of water in the car they had a drink, and handed the rest to those who were to stay behind. In a few minutes the car, running in its own tracks, was purring quietly across the starlit desert.

For a while good progress was made, but then frequent halts became necessary in order to spy out the land ahead, so that the car did not find itself unexpectedly on the enemy aerodrome. In just under an hour, Ginger, convinced that they must be near the enemy camp, went forward on foot to have a look round, and returned with the information that half a mile ahead, in a depression, there was a large oasis in which the enemy base was probably concealed. Under his guidance the car proceeded for half that distance, and then, as there was a risk of its engine being heard, it was stopped in a narrow sandy gully which provided excellent cover, and, incidentally ran on in the direction of the oasis.

At a brief council of war that followed it was decided to leave the car there in charge of Taffy, while Bertie and Ginger, taking the Tommy gun, went forward to scout, and if possible rescue Biggles. Without knowing precisely what lay ahead it was impossible to make detailed plans. The general idea was to find out the lie of the land, rescue Biggles, and return to the car, which would then set out on the long journey to Salima, picking up on the way those waiting by the Whitley.

'You'd better let me go first,' Ginger told Bertie. 'I've had more experience at this sort of thing than you have. I know most of the tricks.'

'Extraordinary fellow,' was Bertie's only comment.

Ginger, revolver in hand, started forward. Visibility was fairly good, but the silence, and the presence of rocks which might hide a sentry, made the advance a slow and anxious task. However, in due course an irregular fringe of palm fronds cutting into the sky revealed the edge of the oasis. An obstruction was also encountered. At the point where the gully fanned out into the oasis a line of tethered camels stood close to a small group of low black tents.

'That must be the Arab camp,' whispered Ginger to Bertie. 'I'd forgotten all about the Toureg the Germans have with them. I can't see anybody on guard.'

'We'd better make a detour,' suggested Bertie.

'That would mean going into the open, and we don't want to do that if it can be avoided. Stand fast.'

With every nerve tense Ginger crept forward, taking advantage of the ample cover provided by the rocks. He reached the camels, most of which, couched for the night, were contentedly chewing the cud, their jaws moving in a steady sideways crunch, left to right, right to left. They looked at Ginger with their great soft eyes, in the human way these animals have, but they showed no sign of alarm. Behind some of them were saddles, and on these lay the cotton nightshirt-like garments worn by Arabs for desert travel. They gave Ginger an idea. He picked one up and threw it across his shoulders so that the ragged ends reached nearly to the ground. As a disguise the robe left much to be desired, but, after all, he reflected, it was dark, and it was better than nothing. He took a *gumbaz*, as these robes are called, back to Bertie, who, with a sniff of disgust, put it on.

'Now let's try our luck in the oasis,' suggested Ginger.

Actually, the approach was easier than they expected, and it seemed that the guard, if one was kept, was not rigidly maintained. They were soon among the palms, walking on coarse dry grass. For a little while they walked on looking about them, for there was nothing to indicate where the actual camp was situated, but eventually a path took them to where a number of lights glowed feebly in the darkness. It was also possible to make out the vague outlines of aircraft, disposed in much the same way as were their own at Salima. A low murmur of conversation came from a large tent some distance to the right, and this, Ginger thought, was the men's quarters. On the left a number of smaller tents were presumably those of the officers. It seemed likely that Biggles would be in one of them, because it was improbable that there could be a permanent building in the oasis.

So far they had seen no human beings, which struck Ginger as strange, and he was wondering what could have happened to the Arabs when from the direction of the large tent a number now appeared. Without speaking they passed on and disappeared in the direction of the camels. One, possibly the leader, remained for a little while talking in low tones to a man in uniform; then he salaamed and walked on after his companions. Ginger was too far away to hear what was said; nor could he make out the nationality of the man in uniform, although he supposed him to be an Italian or a German. This man strode towards the smaller tents.

Ginger waited for him to disappear and then turned to Bertie. 'Stay here for a minute,' he said. 'I'll go over to those tents and try to learn something. Keep behind this bush, then I shall know where you are.'

'Just as you like,' agreed Bertie. 'I'm all of a twitter.'

Keeping among the palms, Ginger made his way to the tents. Not a sound came from any of them, which puzzled him, for he thought that at least a few officers should be about. Then, beyond the tents, he saw a curious arrangement, one that he had to approach and study for some time before he could be fairly sure what it was. He made it out to be a sort of lean-to structure, about thirty feet long, roofed with palm fronds. The front was open in the manner of a barn, but the interior was in such deep shadow that he could not see into it. It was a sentry standing at each end armed with a rifle that gave him an idea of the purpose for which the primitive building was intended. It was the prisoners' quarters. If this surmise was correct, then it seemed probable that Biggles would be there, thought Ginger, as from a thick group of palms he surveyed the scene. Not only Biggles, but the passengers of the air liners that had been shot down. He wondered vaguely how many there were, for this raised a new problem. Naturally, they would all be anxious to be rescued, but this, obviously, was impossible. The next step was to find out if Biggles was there, although just how this was to be achieved was not apparent.

A cautious detour brought him to the rear of the building, where a disappointment awaited him. He had hoped that it might be possible to break a way through, but he found that the rear wall was built of palm trunks, laid one upon the other. To make a hole, even with the proper tools, would be a noisy operation. It seemed that the only way to get into the building was from the front, and this would not be possible without disposing of at least one of the sentries.

He was still pondering the problem, standing at the rear of the building and two or three paces from one end, when a development occurred which at first seemed to provide him with just the opportunity that he required. He could not see the sentries, but suddenly they started a conversation only a few yards from where he stood. It was evident that the sentry at the far end had walked down to have a word with his partner, and this suggested that it should be possible to affect an entry at that end.

Ginger was about to move away when something one of the sentries said made him pause. The man spoke in German, and although Ginger would not have claimed to be able to speak the language fluently, he understood it fairly well, or at least enough to follow a conversation.

'This is an amazing thing about Hauptmann von Zoyton,' said one sentry.

'Yes, it is a mystery,' returned the other.

'I don't understand it,' continued the first speaker.

'Nobody can,' was the reply. 'Everyone saw plain enough what happened. I myself saw him come down on the parachute, and could have sworn he fell into the trees at the far end of the oasis. Everyone thought so. I was one of those who ran to the place, but when we got there there was no sign of him. The Arabs have searched everywhere. I hear they are just going out to make a fresh search in the desert, in case he went that way.'

'But why should he do that?'

'Well, where else could he have gone? He might have been wounded, or perhaps he hurt himself when he landed and didn't know what he was doing. Instead of coming into the oasis he might have wandered away among the dunes.'

'Possibly,' agreed the other sentry. 'Still, it's a queer business. All the officers are still searching for him.'

With what interest Ginger listened to this enlightening conversation can be better imagined than described. It was easy enough to understand what had happened, and he could have kicked himself for not thinking of the possibility. The Germans at the oasis had seen the blue-nosed Messerschmitt shot down, but they were not to know that the man in it was not von Zoyton. They had assumed, naturally, that it was. They had gone to meet him, but he had not been found, for the very good reason that the pilot who had descended by parachute was Biggles, who had managed to find a hiding place before their arrival. It came to this. Biggles had not been taken prisoner. He was still at large, and the Germans did not know, or even suspect, that the man was not their commanding officer. They were still looking for him. This altered the entire situation, and left Ginger wondering what he ought to do about it.

His first decision was to retire, to return to Bertie and get clear of the oasis, leaving Biggles to make his own way home. Two more British officers in the oasis, far from helping him might easily make his task more difficult. Then Ginger had a second thought. The sentry who should be at the far end of the prison hut— if it was a prison hut—had left his post. It should be a simple matter to get in at that end and find out who was inside, information which Biggles would certainly be glad to have. Turning, he started running along the soft sand that had drifted like waves against the back of the building, leaving dark hollows between them. In the very first one of these he stumbled and fell over something soft, something which, he could tell by the feel of it, was alive. With a grunt of alarm he scrambled to rise, but before he could do so a dark form had flung itself on him and borne him to the ground; a vicelike grip closed over his neck, forcing his face into the sand. In another moment, in spite of his desperate struggles, his *gumbaz* was being wrapped round his head, blinding him and suffocating him with its voluminous folds. Then, for no reason that he could imagine, the grip of his assailant relaxed, and the choking rags were torn from his face. Bewildered by the ferocity of the attack, and gasping for breath, he sat up, wondering what had happened and prepared for a renewal of the assault.

'Great Heavens!' breathed a voice.

Ginger stared at the face of the man who stood

bending over him. It was Biggles. His eyes were round with wonder and his expression one of utter disbelief.

'Ginger!' he stammered. 'I thought . . . I thought—you were dead,' he gulped.

'Yes, I know. It wasn't me, though. It was Hymann.'

'If I hadn't used your nightshirt for a gag, and so seen your uniform—'

Ginger, remembering the two sentries, raised a warning finger. He felt sure the scuffle must have been heard; and, sure enough, one of the sentries came round the corner of the hut.

'Is this a free fight?' he inquired humorously, in German.

'Yes,' answered Biggles, in the same language. 'You're just in time.'

There was a crack as his fist met the sentry's jaw, and the man, unprepared for such a reception, went over backwards, the rifle flying from his hands.

'Give me that nightshirt, Ginger,' said Biggles. 'We'd better truss him up before he starts squawking.'

'There's another sentry about somewhere.'

'I fancy he's gone back to his post,' answered Biggles, rising to his feet, looking down on the sentry who, tied up in the *gumbaz*, looked unpleasantly like a corpse.

'Where have you been since I shot you down?' asked Ginger.

'So you've discovered it was me you chose for a target?' returned Biggles, coldly. 'If you want to know, I've been frizzling on the crown of a palm. But don't let's waste time over that—I'll tell you about it later. We've got to get out of this. How did you get here?'

'We grabbed the enemy's car. Bertie is with me.'

'Fine! I could have been outside the oasis by now, but it struck me that while I was here I might as well

104

try to collect General Demaurice. I was lying here when you kindly trod on my face. Where's Bertie?'

'Over by that bush.'

'And the car?'

'In a gully behind the oasis. Taffy is sitting at the wheel.'

'Good! Stand fast. I'm going to see if I can find the General.' Biggles disappeared into the darkness.

In a fever of anxiety Ginger waited. Once or twice there was a buzz of conversation inside the hut, but no alarm was sounded. Then Biggles came back, bringing with him a man whom Ginger recognised as the French General.

'It's tough on the others,' murmured Biggles, as they walked towards the bush where Bertie was waiting, 'but they'll have to wait. We can't take them all.'

'How many prisoners are there?' asked Ginger.

'Fourteen. I told them we'll come back for them as soon as possible.'

They reached the bush. Bertie was astonished.

'I say, old battle-axe, this is wonderful, absolutely marvellous. Congratulations—'

'Save them till we're out of the wood,' cut in Biggles crisply. 'Lead on to the car, Ginger—you know the way.'

'Everything going like clockwork, by Jingo,' declared Bertie, as they came in sight of the car still standing where they had left it.

As he spoke there came shouts that rose to a clamour from the direction of the camp.

'You spoke a bit too soon,' Biggles told Bertie. 'Either they've missed the General, or found the sentry I had to truss up.'

Taffy was there. He beamed when he saw Biggles, and started to say something, but Biggles stopped him.

'Get going,' he said, 'and put your foot on it. I've an idea we've stirred up a hornets' nest.'

As they got into the car, from the direction of the aerodrome came the roar of aircraft engines being started up.

Chapter 9
A Perilous Passage

The car was soon racing back over its trail at a speed that caused the sand to fly, and Ginger to hold his breath, for he remembered Taffy's reputation for breaking things. The wilderness was littered with boulders, and they had only to strike one at the rate they were travelling to end in dire calamity. He mentioned it to Biggles, who, however, thought it better not to distract Taffy's attention from what he was doing.

'The nearer we get to Tex and Tug before the storm hits us the better,' he remarked. 'It's going to be a race, and every second is valuable.'

'Storm? What storm?' asked Bertie.

'The one that will hit us when the Messerschmitts find us,' answered Biggles, grimly. 'You heard the engines being started? They aren't going on a joy-ride, or anything like that. In a minute they'll be looking for us.'

'We're not showing any lights,' Ginger pointed out.

'No matter. They may not spot us while we're in this gully among the rocks; but the moon is coming up, and when we have to cross open sand we shall be as conspicuous as a spider on a whitewashed wall. The Nazis have several machines besides Messerschmitt 109's; I noticed, among others, a Messerschmitt 110* fighter-bomber. If that baby finds us we are likely to have a rousing time.'

* Twin-engined German fighter-bomber with a crew of three.

107

'I'll have a look round to see if I can see anything,' said Ginger, and climbed up the central turret until his head and shoulders were clear above the metal rim.

Overhead, the heavens were a thing to marvel at. Stars gleamed like lamps suspended from a ceiling of dark blue velvet. The rising moon cast an unearthly radiance over the sterile wilderness. He could not see any hostile aircraft—not that he expected to; nor, for some time could he hear anything on account of the noise made by the car; then a sound made him look up, and he saw something that turned his mouth dry with shock. Almost immediately overhead a dark shape suddenly crystallised in the gloom, growing swiftly larger and more distinct. Knowing only too well what it was he let out a yell and tumbled back into the car.

'Look out!' he shouted. 'There's a dive-bomber right on top of us!'

Luckily the car was now running over an area of flat sand, like a dry river bed, and almost before the words had left Ginger's lips Taffy had swung the wheel hard over, causing the car to dry-skid so violently that those inside were flung against each other. An instant later the car swerved again, and nearly overturned, as the blast of a terrific explosion struck it.

'Shall I stop and let you out?' yelled Taffy.

'No—keep going!' shouted Biggles. 'He'll find it harder to hit a moving target than a stationary one. This car's our only chance of getting back—we can't afford to lose it. Keep going towards the rendezvous, but take your orders from me. When I shout "now," turn as sharply as you dare.'

So saying, Biggles ran up into the turret. He saw the attacking machine, a Messerschmitt 110, immediately, for it was flying low. As he expected, it had overshot them, pulling up after its dive, and was now turning steeply for a second effort. He watched it closely, saw it line up behind the speeding car, and put its nose down in a dive that grew swiftly steeper. He waited for the bombs—there were three this time—to detach themselves before shouting 'Now!'

Again the car turned so sharply that he was flung against the side of the turret. He ducked below the rim and waited for the explosions that he knew must come.

Three mighty detonations, coming so close together that they sounded as one, shook the car as if it had been tissue paper. They were followed by a violent spatter, as of hail, as sand and stones smote the armour plate.

'I say, old top, how many of those blessed things does the fellow carry?' asked Bertie, in a pained voice. 'Beastly noise—nearly made me drop my eye-glass.'

'I'll let you know,' answered Biggles, smiling, and returned to his watch tower.

Twice more the aircraft dived, but each time the bombs missed their mark, for which the pilot was not to be blamed, for the fast-moving car did not keep a straight course for a moment.

'I think that's the lot,' said Biggles, watching the Messerschmitt, which after circling, had turned away.

But now two Messerschmitt 109's had arrived on the scene; he guessed that the explosions had brought them to the spot, and knew that they would use their guns.

'Keep going,' he told Taffy. 'You're doing fine. We're more than half way. That bomber may have gone home for some more pills, so we've got to beat it to the rendezvous. In any case, there's a brace of 109's over-head—look out, here they come!' Biggles' voice ended

109

in a shout, and he dropped back into the car, slamming the cover behind him.

A few seconds later a withering blast of bullets struck the metal plating, without piercing it, although the noise was alarming. A tracer cannon shell went clean through the turret like a flash of lightning, but fortunately did no damage. It missed the French General's head by inches, but he only smiled.

'We can't stand much of that,' remarked Ginger.

'You keep swerving,' Biggles told Taffy, 'but keep a general course for the rendezvous. Maybe I can discourage those fellows from being over-zealous.' He picked up the Tommy gun and mounted the turret in time to see a Messerschmitt racing along behind them almost at their own level.

A Tommy gun was not an ideal weapon for his purpose, because it has to be held, accuracy being hardly possible in a moving vehicle; but the stream of bullets which Biggles sent at the pursuing Messerschmitt served a useful purpose in that they made the aircraft turn aside, so that the pilot's aim was spoilt, and the bullets merely kicked up a line of sand. Moreover, evidently realising that he was not shooting at a helpless target, the pilot and his companion turned away and exercised more caution in their attacks.

'What will happen when we get to the rendezvous?' asked Ginger. 'We can't leave Tex and Tug.'

'I don't propose to leave them,' answered Biggles.

'What about the prisoners?'

'We'll decide what to do with them when we get there.'

Biggles climbed down into the car. 'Drive straight in when we get there,' he told Taffy. 'Maybe we can find cover among the rocks till these confounded Messerschmitts get tired of shooting at us, or run out of ammunition. At the rate they've been using it that shouldn't be long.'

Unfortunately, the arrival at the rendezvous coincided with the return of the Messerschmitt 110.

Biggles had just got out of the car, and was walking towards Tex and Tug, who were sitting on either side of the little group of prisoners. Tug had a Tommy gun across his knees, and Tex had pushed his revolver into his belt. All this was clear in the bright moonlight. Bertie, Ginger, Taffy and General Demaurice were filing out of the car to stretch their legs.

Biggles said to Tug, 'Is everything all right?'

Tug said that it was. 'What's this coming?' he asked, staring at the sky towards the north-west from where now came the roar of an aircraft travelling at high speed.

Biggles thought quickly, and for a few seconds without reaching a decision. The approaching machine, coming from that direction, could only be an enemy. The pilot would see the car, or if not the car, the black wreckage of the burnt machines. There was still time to take cover, but the problem was what to do with the prisoners. The car would be the target, and it was a matter of common sense to get away from it.

By this time the aircraft, flying low, was close, and Biggles had to make up his mind quickly. 'Scatter and take cover!' he shouted urgently. 'Get away from the car—General, get amongst the rocks—anywhere—but get away.'

'What about these guys?' Tex indicated his prisoners.

'Take them with you—I'll help you,' answered Biggles, tersely.

But it was not to be as easy as that. A stream of

111

tracer bullets flashed through the air, thudding into the sand and smacking viciously against the rocks.

'Down everybody!' yelled Biggles, and flung himself behind a boulder.

An instant later there came the shrill whine of a bomb. It was short-lived. There was a blinding flash, a deafening roar, and everything was blotted out in a cloud of black smoke and swirling sand.

After that it was everyone for himself. It was impossible to maintain any kind of order. Between bursts of fire and the crash of bombs Ginger sprinted for his life to a tall outcrop of rock, and flung himself at the base. Somebody was already there. It was the German driver of the car. Ginger ignored him; at that moment he was not concerned with prisoners. The noise was appalling; bombs exploded and machine guns crackled against a background of aircraft engines. There was obviously more than one machine now, and looking up Ginger could see three, circling low and turning to fire at the stationary car. What with the noise, and the glittering lines of tracer shells and bullets, the place was an inferno. The air was full of sand, which made breathing difficult. Where the others were, and what they were doing, he had no idea, but he was terribly afraid that casualties were going to be heavy unless they had got well clear of the car.

Suddenly the roar of engines increased to a terrifying crescendo, and the air seemed to be full of machines. Ginger could count six, and at first he thought they were all Messerschmitts; then one swept low over him and he could see from the silhouette of its wings that it was a Spitfire. He could only suppose that Algy, or Ferocity, or Henry, or all three, had arrived from Salima. The machines began to shoot at each other, and Ginger watched spellbound the firework display thus provided. It gave some relief to those on the ground, for as they fought, the opposing machines climbed. In one respect Ginger thought, the Spitfires held the advantage. The Germans must have used up most of their ammunition before the British machines had arrived on the scene. An aircraft—Spitfire or Messerschmitt he could not tell—burst into flames, and crashing among the rocks gave a finishing touch to the lurid scene. Then for a little while the noise of engines receded, presently to increase again in volume as three machines—all Spitfires—came tearing back. Ginger knew then it could only be Algy, Ferocity and Henry.

For a minute or two the machines circled and then departed in a south-easterly direction. Ginger saw a figure stand up not far away and recognised Biggles. He ran over to him.

'They're going home,' he said, pointing to the Spitfires.

'Yes. They were quite right not to risk a night landing at a place like this,' answered Biggles. 'Gosh! What a party! I think it's all over. Where's everybody?' Cupping his hands round his mouth he shouted, 'Hi! Where are you?'

Dark figures, some near and some far, began to appear out of the settling sand. Bertie arrived first.

'I say, you fellows,' he said in a worried voice, 'have you seen my bally eyeglass—I've lost it?'

'Don't be a fool,' snapped Biggles, 'it's in your eye.'

'Well I'm dashed! Do you know, I never thought of looking there,' murmured Bertie, apologetically.

Taffy came, limping. He had been wounded in the leg by a bullet, but he said it was only a scratch.

The General came, brushing sand off his uniform

113

and muttering his opinion of the Nazis in a low voice. He had lost his cap.

Biggles spotted a body lying in a grotesque position on the ground, and ran to it to discover that it was the German driver. He was stone dead, shot through the head. Tug came, staggering. He had, he said, been flung against a rock by blast, and knocked out. He was all right now. Tex came running from the desert.

'I've lost the prisoners,' he said.

Biggles pointed to the dead man. 'There's one,' he observed. 'What happened to the rest?'

'I've no idea,' admitted Tex. 'I was close to them when a bomb smothered us with sand. When it cleared they weren't in sight.'

'It doesn't matter, except that I should have liked to keep von Zoyton,' muttered Biggles. 'Naturally, he'd grab the chance to get away. I'm glad things are no worse. That was a Messerschmitt that crashed—we can't do anything about it. Let's go and look at the car.'

It had not, after all, received a direct hit from a bomb, although there were several craters near it, and as well as being half smothered with sand it was tilted on one side. Their combined efforts were required to right it. The plating had been pierced by several cannon shells.

'Good thing we didn't stay in it,' observed Biggles, dryly. 'The thing that really matters is the engine. Get in, Taffy, and try it. If the engine works the car will still be serviceable, and I'd rather ride than walk. We're a long way from home.'

The engine started without any trouble at all, much to Biggles' satisfaction.

'All right, we'll see about getting home,' he

114

announced. 'The Messerschmitts will be out after us again as soon as it gets light. They'll probably come here first, and seeing the car gone will know we've got away. They'll follow our tracks, no doubt, but that can't be prevented.'

'What about having a look round for von Zoyton?' suggested Ginger.

'We can't stop to look for him now—not that we'd ever find him in the dark amongst all this rock. His people will pick him up in the morning.'

They all got into the car which, with Taffy still at the wheel, resumed its journey across the desert.

'Our jolly little plan seems to have come unstuck this time,' murmured Bertie.

'You mean *my* plan,' answered Biggles. 'I get the credit when things go right, so I'll take the kicks when they go wrong. This time it didn't work out. Plans don't always work out, you know. If mine never went wrong I shouldn't be a man, I'd be a magician; and, moreover, I should have won the war long ago. Actually, the thing hasn't worked out as badly as it might have done. It was that skunk Hymann bolting that upset the apple cart. How did he get away, Ginger?'

Ginger told the story of the Nazi's escape.

'Well, he didn't get far,' remarked Biggles. 'He'd have done better to have kept his parole.'

'What happened to you when I shot you down over the enemy aerodrome?' inquired Ginger. 'I have a rough idea because I heard the German sentries talking, but I'd be interested to hear the details.

'Yes, tell us,' prompted Tex.

'It isn't much of a story,' replied Biggles. Then he burst out laughing. 'I'll tell you something that'll make you smile. When I saw Ginger roaring up in the Spitfire—although, of course, I didn't know it was him at the time—I went to meet him. Believe it or not, I clean forgot I was flying a Messerschmitt. I behaved as though I was flying my own machine, but fortunately I remembered just in time. When the Spitfire made the opening moves I wondered for a moment who the fellow in it was going to attack. I imagined there must be another machine behind me. It wasn't until it came straight at me that I remembered that I was flying a Messerschmitt. You should have seen me get out of the way! The position was a bit difficult because I couldn't shoot back, and had I simply bolted the Spit would have had a sitting target. While I was circling, wondering how I could let the Spit know that I was in the Messer, he made a sieve of my tail unit, and I had to bale out in a hurry. As I floated down it suddenly occurred to me that the Boches might make the same mistake. They must have seen what happened, and would naturally suppose that it was von Zoyton in the blue-nosed aircraft.'

'As a matter of fact, they did think it was von Zoyton,' put in Ginger.

'So I gather,' continued Biggles. 'Before I touched down I had decided to hide if I could find a place. My idea was to wait until dark and then try to get home. I thought I might be able to get hold of another Messerschmitt, or, failing that, pinch a camel from a line which I could see at the far end of the oasis. But it didn't come to that. By what at first I took to be a rotten bit of luck my brolly* hooked up in the top of a palm. There are some tall ones, sixty or seventy feet high, for a guess, at Wadi Umbo—that's the name of

* Slang: parachute.

116

the German camp, by the way. As I say, I got hooked up, and there I hung. Then I saw that really this would be a slice of pie if I could climb up the shrouds of my brolly to the top of the palm. Somehow I managed it, and I'd just pulled the fabric together when the Nazis arrived, looking for me—or rather, for von Zoyton. I sat in the top of the palm like a caterpillar in a cabbage, listening to the Nazis talking underneath. Was it hot! I chewed a date or two and passed the time knotting the shrouds together so that I could get down without breaking my neck when the Nazis got tired of playing hide and seek.'

'No wonder they couldn't make out what had happened to you,' grinned Ginger.

'Yes, it must have seemed odd. Remember, I didn't touch the ground, so there wasn't even a footprint. Nobody ever did the disappearing trick better. Well, I sat there until it got dark; then I made my way to the camp, which, as a matter of detail, was fairly easy, because everybody was out looking for me—or, as they supposed, for von Zoyton. It struck me that it would be a good thing if I could carry away a mental picture of the place, for future use, which I did, making a note of what machines they had, where they were parked, where the dumps were and so on. They've a mobile wireless station. Incidentally, they've got a Rapide there, all complete, as far as I could make out. It must have landed intact. I didn't try to get away in it because that would have been a bit too much of a job single handed. It then occurred to me that as the general is an important officer I ought to try to get them home. I found the so-called prison hut, and was lying at the back waiting for a chance to crack the sentry on the skull, when what I took to be an Arab came stalking along. I couldn't make out what his game was. Of course, it was Ginger, who seems to have developed a knack of turning up at unexpected places, but I didn't know that then. He prowled about for a bit, and then started running along the back of the hut as though he was in a hurry to get somewhere.'

'I was,' interposed Ginger. 'I was making for the far end of the hut, hoping to find out what was inside.'

'Instead of which you put your heel in my mouth,' said Biggles, amid another shout of laughter. 'We had a beautiful wrestle there, all to ourselves. I got the best of it, and was pulling a bunch of stinking rags off my Arab to make a gag when I saw the uniform underneath. And there, as large as life, was Ginger, looking scared stiff, with his face all covered with sand. It takes a lot to shake me, but I don't mind admitting that when I saw Ginger's face I nearly passed out. I don't believe in ghosts, but I thought I'd grabbed one. Naturally, I thought it was Ginger in the Spit that crashed—we all did. But for a ghost this one seemed pretty solid. Moreover, it spluttered.'

'You nearly choked me,' said Ginger indignantly, amid more titters of mirth.

'You don't know how right you are,' replied Biggles warmly. 'I was feeling sort of peeved at the time.' He turned to Taffy. 'How are we getting on?'

'Pretty good.'

'Keep going. It must be nearly dawn. I'll—' Biggles broke off short as from somewhere near at hand came the staccato buzzing of Morse. His eyes followed the sound to its source, and with a quick movement he flung open a panel in the side of the car. 'Radio, by japers!' he cried. 'Two-way radio, at that. I should have known that a car like this would be fitted with it.' He snatched up a pencil from the pad that lay beside the instrument and jotted down the signal as it came through. Half a minute later it stopped abruptly, and he smiled lugubriously at a meaningless jumble of letters that he had written.

'It's in code,' he said ruefully. 'It might be British, it might be German—we've no means of knowing. In any case, without the key it would take an expert to decode it.'

'Doesn't it mean anything to you?' asked Ginger.

'Not a thing. It may be nothing to do with us. The message was not intended for the car, that's certain, because the Nazis know we've got it; we just happened to intercept it. I'll go upstairs and see where we are.' Leaving the radio panel open, he mounted the turret.

Chapter 10
The Haboob

The car was travelling over gentle undulations of sand from the top of which occasionally broke through, like rotten teeth, boulders of bleached rock. The fiery rays of the remorseless sun were just shooting up over the eastern horizon, edging the rocks with a curious incandescent glow and casting weird, elongated shadows behind them. Sky and desert were both the same colour, a dull, venomous red. A hot wind was blowing, carrying little eddies of sand before it.

Even as Biggles watched, a strong gust shook the car, and the sky, instead of becoming lighter, darkened. He had seen the phenomenon before, and knew what was coming—the dreaded *haboob* of the African deserts. His face was grave as he dropped back into the car and faced the others, who, seeing from his face that something was wrong, looked at him questioningly.

'How much water have we?' asked Biggles.

A quick search was made. 'None,' answered Ginger.

Biggles frowned. 'Surely this car didn't start off without water?'

'As a matter of fact there was a can,' explained Ginger. 'But I took it out and left it with the others when Bertie and I went off to look for you at Wadi Umbo. What with the bombing and one thing and another, it must have been left behind. I'm sorry about that.'

'You will be,' promised Biggles grimly. 'A *haboob* is

on the way. It may hit us at any moment. Taffy, keep the car going as long as you can.'

'Do you mean this *haboob* thing can stop a car?' said Tex wonderingly. 'I don't get it.'

'You will,' replied Biggles. 'Get some rag to tie over your faces—use your shirts if there's nothing else. Keep the mouth and nose covered.' Biggles went to the radio and dropped his right hand on the transmitting key.

'What are you going to do?' asked Ginger in surprise.

'Send a signal to Wadi Umbo,'

'To—the Nazis?' cried Ginger incredulously.

'You heard me.'

'Why, in the name of goodness?'

'You haven't forgotten we left our prisoners in the desert?'

'But they bolted.'

'That may be, but we are responsible for planting them there. They can't have got back yet. In fact, I doubt if they'd try. They'd wait for help. Wadi Umbo may not have seen what's coming. I'm going to tell them to pick up von Zoyton and the others.'

'Why bother?' snorted Tex.

'Because it's one thing to shoot a man in a scrap, but a horse of a different colour to drop him in the sand and leave him to the mercy of a *haboob*. Only a skunk would do a thing like that.'

'I reckon a Nazi would do it,' sneered Tex.

'Possibly,' agreed Biggles coldly. 'But it happens that I'm not a Nazi.'

His hand began to move, tapping out the message. With curious eyes the others watched, reading the signal as he sent it out:

From officer commanding R.A.F. to officer commanding

121

Luftwaffe, Wadi Umbo. Haboob coming your way. Pick up four prisoners lost at point approximately thirty miles south-east your position. Prisoners include von Zoyton and Pallini. Confirm signal received. Message ends.

Biggles, a faint smile on his face, waited. A minute later the instrument buzzed the answer in English.

Officer commanding Luftwaffe, Libyan Desert Patrol, to officer commanding R.A.F. Confirming message received . . . confirming message received. Message ends.

Bertie looked pained. 'Rude feller.'

Tex grunted. 'Didn't this guy von Zoyton ever have a mother to teach him to say thank you?'

'Von Zoyton didn't send that signal,' answered Biggles. 'He's still out in the desert. Keep going, Taffy. We may find ourselves in a jam if we can't get through.'

'I say, old boy, you don't seriously mean that a jolly old dust storm can stop a locomotive like this?' inquired Bertie.

'That's just what I do jolly well mean,' answered Biggles sarcastically. 'Even with water that would be serious. Without it—well, things may be grim.'

Biggles sat down and peered through the letter-box slit that gave the driver a view ahead. The sky grew darker, and in a few minutes the car was running through a howling chaos of wind that tore up whirling clouds of sand in its fury. Everything was moving. Sandhills disappeared before the eyes and piled up in another place. Sand poured along the ground in waves, like a rolling sea, crests smoking. Against them the car made little progress. Sand was everywhere. It poured in through the slit and trickled through the roof. Taffy,

122

choking, clung to the wheel with dogged ferocity, but presently the car gave a jolt and stopped.

'That's it.' There was a note of resignation in Biggles' voice. 'We've hit a heap of sand, or jammed in a trough.'

The others looked at him. They did not speak, for to open the mouth was to have it filled with sand. Already the sand gritted in Ginger's teeth. Sand was in his eyes, his ears. It ran down his neck in little streams. He could see it trickling in through the joints of the armour plating. The heat was unbelievable. He remembered that he still had his goggles, so he put them on and looked through the slit. He caught his breath at the sight that met his eyes. The whole landscape was heaving. Above it hung the sun, brown, blurred, swollen, horrible. Wind screamed. Eddies rushed along the ground, whirling upwards, twisting, writhing, piling sand against the car. Dunes rose and fell like a storm-tossed ocean, the tops tumbling and smoking like miniature volcanos. It was no longer possible to see the actual ground. The heat increased until it seemed to be beyond human endurance. It was as though a mighty furnace had burst and set the earth on fire.

Ginger turned away. His face felt raw, his nostrils smarted, his skin itched, and his eyes were dry and sore.

'We're being buried,' he told Biggles in a choking voice. 'The sand is piling up on the car.'

'I was afraid of it,' said Biggles, who had tied a handkerchief over the lower part of his face. 'The car is filling with sand, too.'

'Is there nothing we can do about it?'

'Nothing. It's just one of those things . . . fortunately,

the door is on the leeward side, so we may be able to open it when the storm has passed. There will be tons of sand piled on the windward side.'

'Gosh! I could do with a drink,' panted Tex. 'My tongue's like a file.'

'Don't talk about that,' muttered Biggles curtly. 'If you start thinking about a drink you'll go crazy.'

After that nothing more was said for what seemed an eternity of time, although Biggles knew from his watch that it was really only just over two hours. Then the noise outside began to subside.

'It's passing,' he announced.

Yet not for another half-hour did they attempt to open the door, and then it was only opened with difficulty. One thing was immediately clear. The car would take them no farther. Sand was piled high all round it; on the windward side it reached to the roof. Spades would be required before the car could be freed of its gritty bed. Sand was still settling on it. If the heat inside had been bad, outside it was intolerable. It was obvious that everyone was suffering from thirst, but no one mentioned it.

'I guess we may as well start walking,' suggested Tex.

Biggles did not answer. He was thinking. He was by no means sure of where they were, for the whole face of the desert had altered, but he knew they must still be some distance from the oasis. Of one thing he was certain. If they tried to reach the oasis on foot, without water, they would perish. The end would be the same whether they stayed or went on, he reflected, and had just decided to walk on and meet death rather than wait for it when the buzzer started tapping out a message.

They all stiffened, listening. Biggles took a pace nearer.

'It's in English,' he said, as he heard the first word. 'That means it's for us.'

Letter by letter the message came through:

Hauptmann von Zoyton, Oasis Wadi Umbo, to Squadron Leader Bigglesworth, in Luftwaffe car Z 4421. If you need water there is reserve tank in rear section. Tap under medical chest. I look forward to shooting you. Message ends.

Biggles ran into the car, and dragging aside a seat under the Red Cross cabinet, exposed to view a small metal tap. He turned it, and smelt the liquid that gushed out. 'It's water,' he told the others. 'Help yourselves, but don't overdo it. Empty the bottles in the medicine chest and fill them with water. Fill every vessel you can find.'

He went to the radio transmitter and tapped out a signal:

Squadron Leader Bigglesworth, operating Luftwaffe car Z 4421, to Hauptmann von Zoyton. Message received. Have your guns ready. Will be calling shortly. Message ends.

He turned to the others, who had paused in their drinking to watch him. 'You'll sometimes find,' he averred, 'that if you throw a crust of bread on the water you get a slice back. Without this water we were all dead men. If we hadn't saved von Zoyton he couldn't have saved us. Evidently he has reached Wadi Umbo and learned that we gave his squadron his position. Fill up these bottles and let's get along.'

Having drunk their fill, and carrying a good supply of water in bottles, they struck off across the burning wilderness.

For a little while they were tortured by sand that still hung in the air; then, as it settled, and the sky cleared, the sun flamed down as if to blind them with its rays. The ground threw up a heat so fierce that it created a sensation of wading through liquid rather than air. They trudged on mechanically, in silence, realising that without constant sips of water they could not have lived.

There were many places where the desert had completely changed. Sometimes the sand had been piled up in fantastic dunes; sometimes it had been torn away, leaving the bedrock exposed. Once they had to stumble over a ridge of volcanic clinker that crunched beneath their feet with a noise of breaking crockery, throwing up an acrid dust.

They had covered some miles, and Biggles was sure that they could be no great distance from the oasis, when the unmistakable drone of aircraft was heard behind them. He turned and looked, but as yet he could see nothing.

'Coming from that direction they must be Messerschmitts,' he said. 'They're probably looking for the car.'

Presently they saw an aircraft, too small for the type to be recognised, although as it came from the northwest they knew it must be an enemy machine. Flying at a tremendous height it passed right over.

'Funny he didn't see us,' remarked Ginger.

'We may not notice it, but there's still enough sand in the air to affect visibility,' explained Biggles. 'If they see Salima Oasis they'll guess that's where we came from.'

'They've probably worked that out by now, anyway,' asserted Biggles. 'The oasis is shown on the map. They will know we must be at an oasis, and there aren't many around here. Salima is one of the best—that's why I chose it.' He glanced up. 'That sounds like more machines coming.'

For some while they walked on in silence, with the drone of high flying aircraft in their ears.

'I should say that first machine spotted the oasis and has called up the others,' opined Biggles.

'If they find it they'll shoot it up,' said Ginger.

'Of course they will.'

'In that case I imagine we shall shoot them up?'

'That's just the trouble, we can't,' disputed Biggles. 'There happens to be a number of British prisoners at Wadi Umbo. We daren't risk blitzing our own people.'

From far ahead came the grunting of machine guns, punctuated with the heavier explosions of cannon.

'They're either shooting up Salima now, or else Algy has spotted them and gone out to meet them,' said Biggles. He strode on, his eyes on the sky ahead.

'There's somebody going down—look!' cried Ginger suddenly, as a plume of black smoke fell diagonally across the sky.

Biggles did not answer. He walked on, with the others trailing behind him. Slowly the noise of aircraft died away and silence fell. Soon afterwards the palms of the oasis came into sight. Wearily they strode towards it.

Chapter 11
Happenings at Salima

Half an hour later, dizzy from the blinding heat, they reached the oasis to find, as Biggles had feared, that the enemy had discovered their camp and shot it up. After drinking, and plunging their faces in water, in the welcome shade of the mess tent Algy told them what had happened. He was more than a little relieved to see them. They all knew about the night battle, so he skipped it, and narrated the events of the morning.

He said that he had intended—naturally—to take off at the crack of dawn to look for them, and he, Henry and Ferocity were actually taxying out when the *haboob* hit the oasis and threw everything into confusion. Not only was flying out of the question, but it was only by strenuous efforts by all hands that the machines had been saved. As soon as the air was reasonably clear, he, with Ferocity and Henry—it turned out that he had not been badly hurt by Hymann's blow—had got out the machines again to make a reconnaissance. They had food and water ready to drop if it was needed. They guessed the car would be stranded.

At this moment, when the Spitfires were taxying out to take off, a Messerschmitt had suddenly appeared over the oasis. They had not heard it coming because their engines were running. This Messerschmitt had at once radioed its discovery to Wadi Umbo, and to other machines that were out looking for the car, giving the position of Salima. They knew this because the message had been picked up by Corporal Roy Smyth who was on duty at the time; but it was only when the flight sergeant ran up with the news that he, Algy, knew that an attack on the oasis was imminent. Thereafter things had happened fast. Messerschmitts seemed to come from all directions. Algy had counted six, as, with Ferocity and Henry, he took off to give battle. By this time the Messerschmitts were diving on the oasis shooting it up with their guns.

In the dog fight that followed Algy had shot down one Messerschmitt in flames, and Ferocity had driven another into the ground, both the enemy pilots being killed. Henry had badly damaged another Messerschmitt before being shot down himself. He had baled out and was unhurt, but his machine was a total wreck. Both the other Spitfires had been damaged, but they were being repaired and were already serviceable if required. On the ground two airmen had been wounded. A certain amount of damage had been done to stores, but the petrol dumps had escaped.

Biggles, and those who had come in from the desert, listened to this recital without speaking. When it was finished Biggles said: 'It might have been worse; in fact, you seem to have got out of the mess pretty well. We can't expect to have things all our own way and this was certain to happen sooner or later. Now von Zoyton knows where we are, and he was bound to find that out eventually, things are likely to start buzzing. We are still on the credit side, but I'm not very happy about the position. We mustn't lose sight of the fact that this private war with von Zoyton is only incidental to our job of keeping the route clear. Let's see, how do we stand for machines?'

'We are down to three Spits, actually at the oasis,'

answered Algy. 'Originally we had six. We've lost two by enemy action, and Bertie's is still at Karga, where he left it when he went to fetch the Whitley. We've also lost the Whitley. There are four Spitfires and a Defiant at Karga. We'd better see about getting them over.'

'Yes, but how? Angus is alone at Karga. The machines won't fly themselves here, and we've no transport to send people to Karga. It can be done by using the Defiant, but it will take time. In the meanwhile, if another machine starts across the route, and gets lost, my name will be mud with the Air Ministry. They don't care two hoots about our troubles. All they're concerned with is the machines getting through—and quite rightly. It's this blessed compass juggling that worries me. We've got to put a stop to that, or none of our machines will get through.'

'Three of us could fly the three Spits to Karga with passengers on our laps,' suggested Ginger.

'And leave the oasis without any air defence? We should be in a lovely mess if von Zoyton came over—as he will—and we hadn't a single machine here. No, that won't do. I've got to get General Demaurice to Egypt, too.'

The General, who had not so far spoken, even when the car had been stranded in the desert, stepped into the conversation. 'Why not send a radio message to Egypt, for more machines and pilots? Surely they would let you have them?'

'They might,' agreed Biggles. 'And thanks, Monsieur le General, for the suggestion. But that isn't quite our way of doing things. I was given enough men and machines to do this job and I aim to do it. If I can't the Higher Command will jolly soon relieve me of my command. I have a two-seater at Karga. I propose to send for it. One of my pilots will fly you to the nearest point from where you will be able to get to Cairo. I'd be obliged if you would carry my despatches with you.'

'I am entirely at your service, monsieur,' said the General.

'Thank you.' Biggles turned to Flight Sergeant Smyth, who was waiting for orders. 'Wireless-silence doesn't matter any longer now the enemy knows we're here. Send a signal to Mr. Mackail and ask him to fly the Defiant here right away.'

'Very good, sir.' The flight sergeant departed.

'What we really need for transport purposes is the Rapide von Zoyton has got at Wadi Umbo,' remarked Ginger wishfully.

Biggles whistled softly. 'By jingo! That's an idea,' he said slowly. 'I wonder . . . ?'

For a minute Biggles remained lost in thought. Then he looked up. 'That's all for the present,' he said. 'You had better all go and get some rest. Bertie, Taffy and Tex, I shall have to ask you to be duty pilots in case any trouble blows along. You can sleep, but stay by your machines and keep your clothes on. I'll arrange for reliefs in two hours.'

Algy and Ginger lingered after the others had gone. 'You two had better go and get some sleep, too,' advised Biggles. He smiled. 'I may want you to-night.'

'Got an idea?' asked Algy shrewdly.

The flight sergeant came in with a slip of paper. 'Signal from Egypt just in, sir. I've decoded it. A machine is leaving for the West Coast at dawn tomorrow.'

Biggles took the signal. 'That's torn it,' he muttered. 'Now I've *got* to think of something between now and to-morrow morning. If this machine doesn't get

131

through it will mean a rap over the knuckles for me, from headquarters.'

'Perhaps the Nazis won't know about this machine starting?' suggested Ginger hopefully. 'After all, the signal is in code. They can't read it even if they pick it up.'

'We may safely assume that they'll learn about it in the same way that they learned about the other machines. Their Intelligence must be providing them with the information.'

'You mean a spy is letting them know?'

'Yes—apparently.'

'Couldn't we find this fellow?'

'That isn't our job. It might take weeks, and what do you suppose is going to happen in the meantime? Never mind about that now. Go and get some sleep. I've some writing to do before I can have a nap. Flight sergeant, let me know if you hear aircraft approaching.' Biggles sat down at the table and began to write.

When, four hours later, the flight sergeant went in to report the approach of the Defiant, he found Biggles sound asleep.

Flight-Lieutenant Angus Mackail taxied in and jumped down.

Biggles was waiting for him. 'You've been a long time getting here, Angus,' he greeted.

'My boys were doing a top overhaul when your signal arrived,' explained Angus. 'I got away as quickly as I could. What's been going on? Where's everybody?'

'Sleeping,' answered Biggles. 'Things have started to warm up. It's a long story—I'll tell you about it later. We're up against rather a tough proposition. We've lost the Whitley. You've got four Spits at Karga, I believe?'

'Aye, that's right.'

'I shall need them, but for the moment I have a job for you. I have a French General here who must be got to Egypt right away. Our nearest point of contact with a communication squadron able to provide transport to Cairo is Wadi Halfa. I want you to fly the General there and then come back here as quickly as possible. Wadi Halfa is the best part of five hundred miles, which means nearly a thousand miles for the round trip. I reckon you ought to be back here by sunset. It's a bit of a sweat for you—'

'Dinna worry about that, laddie,' broke in Angus. 'Gi'e me the General, and let's get awa'. I'll be glad to be doing something. I seem to have been missing the fun.'

'No doubt there'll still be some fun—as you call it—when you get back. Your boys will be all right at Karga?'

'Aye. I left the sergeant in charge.'

'Good. I'll fetch the General.'

The General, who was asleep, was awakened. Biggles gave him an envelope, requesting him to deliver it to British Air Headquarters, Middle East. Then, as there was no reason for delay, the Defiant took off, heading due east.

Biggles watched it go, and then turned to find that the noise of the aircraft had awakened most of those who were sleeping. He beckoned to Algy and Ginger and took them to the mess tent. 'I want a word with you,' he said.

When they were inside he sat down and continued. 'To-night I'm going to scotch the wireless beam at Wadi Umbo,' he announced calmly. 'It's the first thing to be done if we're going to make the route reasonably

133

safe—I mean, it's no earthly use machines trying to get through while their compasses are going gaga. They'd get off their course, anyhow, and probably run out of petrol even if they weren't shot down by von Zoyton's crowd.'

'Did you see the electrical gear when you were at Wadi Umbo?' asked Algy.

'Yes. It's mobile, of course—two big lorries side by side with an aerial stretched between two lopped-off palms. Unfortunately they are near the prisoners quarters, so we daren't shoot them up for fear of hitting our own people. The job will have to be done on the ground.'

'In other words you're going to the oasis to blow the works up?' put in Ginger.

'That's the idea. If things go well we may be able to kill one or two other birds with the same stone. We might get the Rapide, and the prisoners at the same time. We could then plaster the oasis, a pleasure at present denied us because of the prisoners there. I'm telling you about this now because I may need some help. We've done so many shows together, and know each others methods so well, that I'd rather have you with me than anybody. Some of the others may be in it too. I'm just working out the details of the scheme. I'll get everybody together later on and we'll go into it. We shall need the Defiant. Angus has taken General Demaurice to Wadi Halfa, but I hope he'll be back by sunset. That's all for the moment. I thought I'd just warn you of what I had in mind. In any case, I felt that we ought to be doing something. It's no use just sitting here waiting for von Zoyton to come over to us—as he will, you may be sure, because he must be feeling pretty sore. I was never much good at fighting

134

a defensive war, anyway.' Biggles got up. 'Let's go and
have some lunch and get all the rest we can. We shan't
have much to-night.'

Chapter 12
The Enemy Strikes Again

Biggles was restless, as a commander must be when he knows that a superior force is within striking distance. As the afternoon wore on he walked often to the fringe of the oasis and gazed long and steadily into the north-western sky. He had an uneasy feeling that von Zoyton's *jagdstaffel*, with the advantage of a bomber at its disposal, would be over again before he was in a position to hit back. If von Zoyton was the commander that rumour gave him out to be, he must know, as Biggles knew, that in air warfare offensive tactics alone can bring success. Biggles was being forced temporarily to the defensive, and he did not like it. He hoped that the Nazi ace would hold his hand until he, Biggles, could strike.

That von Zoyton, now aware of his presence at Salima, would be as anxious to wipe him out, as he, Biggles, was to put the Nazi station out of action, could not be doubted, particularly as a civil aircraft was due to go through in the morning. Biggles even considered sending a signal to Egypt asking that the proposed flight be delayed; but on second thoughts he dismissed the idea. It would look too much like weakness – or inefficiency. Von Zoyton would guess, correctly, that the civil aircraft would be escorted through the danger zone by Spitfires, so if he could keep the Spitfires on the ground he would certainly do so.

Thus Biggles reasoned, putting himself in the Nazi

commander's place. But for the British prisoners at Wadi Umbo, he would, even with the limited force at his disposal, have carried out an offensive patrol over the enemy camp, but he dare not risk killing the prisoners there.

However, even with these thoughts on his mind, Biggles did not waste time, but kept every man on the station as hard at work as the heat would permit, digging trenches for cover against bombs and piling sand around the store dumps. Apart from the three Spitfires he had no defence against air attack. The machine he feared most was the Messerschmitt 110, a formidable three-seater fighter-bomber, capable of doing an immense amount of damage. As far as he knew, von Zoyton had only one, for which he was thankful. The oasis was an easy target to find, yet owing to the heat of the sun he dare not move either men or machines out of it. If the bomber came over they would have to take what came down—part from what the three Spitfires could do to prevent the bomber from operating with accuracy. He knew roughly when the enemy would come over—if they were coming.

'I don't think they'll come in the heat of the day,' he told Flight-Sergeant Smyth, who had followed him round the camp on a final inspection. 'Von Zoyton will hardly expect to attack us without suffering some damage, and if he's as clever as I think he is, he won't risk subjecting his pilots to a possible forced landing on the homeward journey, knowing that anyone so landing would probably die of thirst before help could reach him. If he's coming it will be just before sundown; then anyone cracking up between here and Wadi Umbo would have a chance to get home in the cool of the

137

night. If anything starts, blow your whistle. That will be the signal for the men to take cover. There's nothing else we can do. They understand that?'

'Yes, sir.'

'Lord Lissie and Mr. O'Hara will fly the Spitfires with me if trouble starts.'

'So I understand, sir.'

Biggles lit a cigarette and strolled back to the northern fringe of the oasis. In the west, the sun was sinking like a big red toy balloon towards the horizon, and he began to hope seriously that von Zoyton was not coming—at any rate, before Angus in the Defiant got back. That would give him another machine.

As events turned out, this hope was not to be fulfilled. His surmise regarding von Zoyton's tactics was correct. A hum, so slight as to be almost inaudible, reached his ears, and he gave an exclamation of annoyance. For a moment he stood staring up at the sky, but seeing nothing he turned and raced towards his machine.

In the camp the flight-sergeant's whistle shrilled.

When Biggles reached his aircraft Bertie and Tex were already in their machines, their airscrews whirling.

'Watch my tail, as far as you can!' he shouted as he slipped into his parachute harness. 'If the bomber is there I'm going to get it.'

With that he swung himself into the cockpit, started the engine, taxied tail-up to the open sand and swept like a winged torpedo into the air. As he climbed steadily for height, swinging round towards the north-west, a glance in the reflector showed the two other Spitfires close behind him.

He now concentrated his attention on the sky, seeking the enemy, and soon made out two Me. 109's flying together at about eight thousand feet. To the three Spitfires they may have looked, as no doubt they were intended to look, easy victims; but Biggles was not deceived by so transparent a ruse. Long experience, amounting almost to instinct, made him lift his eyes to the sky overhead, and it did not take him long to spot four more Me. 109's flying in line ahead at about ten thousand feet above the two lower machines.

'Six,' he mused. 'That's probably the lot. Von Zoyton can't have many machines left.'

But even now he was not satisfied. Where was the bomber? He felt certain that if it was serviceable von Zoyton would use it, because one well-placed bomb might do more damage to the oasis than all the single-seaters. But where was it?

Keyed up now for the fight that was inevitable, he half turned in his seat and studied the air below him. For a moment he saw nothing; then a movement far below, on the far side of the oasis, caught his eye, and he recognized the sinister shape of the Me. 110. The six fighters were obviously intended to attract attention to themselves while the bomber did its work. That was why, Biggles realized, the fighters had as yet made no move towards him, although they must have seen him. They were trying to draw him away from the oasis.

Turning his tail to the Nazi fighters he streaked for the bomber, now steepening its dive towards its target. It was some distance away, and he hardly hoped to reach it before it dropped its first bomb, but he thought he might get close enough to upset the pilot's aim. A swift glance behind and upward showed the six Messerschmitts, their ruse having failed, coming down behind him—the top four almost vertically. Bertie and Tex were turning to meet them.

Biggles was sorry to leave the two Spitfires, but the destruction of the bomber was imperative if the oasis was not to be blitzed out of existence, and he might never get a better chance. His lips tightened to a thin line as, with his eyes on the bomber, he held his control column forward in a power-dive as steep as the aircraft would stand. The bomber was still going down, too, apparently unaware of his presence.

It may have been that one of the gunners in the bomber actually helped him by calling his pilot's attention to him by opening fire. Tracers streamed upwards, cutting glittering white lines through the air between the two machines; but the range was still too long for effective shooting, and Biggles merely increased the pressure of his right foot on the rudder-bar so that the Spitfire swerved just enough to take it clear of the bullets. At the same time the pilot of the Me. 110, who must have heard the guns at the rear of his own machine, looked up and saw death coming like a meteor—at least, so Biggles supposed, for the bomber started to turn away, dropping a stick of bombs that fell harmlessly across the area of sand that had been used for a landing ground.

This told Biggles much. He knew that the rear gunner was new to the business, probably a beginner, or he would have held his fire; and the pilot's swerve indicated clearly that he was nervous. Biggles acted accordingly, deliberately adding to the enemy pilot's anxiety by firing a short burst, not so much with any real hope of hitting the bomber as to 'rattle' the pilot.

The Nazi responded as Biggles hoped he would—in fact, as he was almost sure he would. In a not unnatural desire to save his life, or at any rate improve his position, he abandoned his target and tried to get under the protective curtain of the 109's. From his erratic flying it was apparent that he was flustered. A fleeting glance in his reflector showed Biggles three of the 109's engaged with Bertie and Tex, while the other three came tearing down on his tail to save the bomber. Clearly, he would have to finish the bomber before they reached him.

At this moment the pilot of the Me. 110 made a blunder which brought a bleak smile to Biggles' lips. He started to climb steeply towards his comrades, losing speed accordingly, and offering an easier target. Biggles was travelling at a rate that jammed his head tight against the head-rest. His zoom at the bottom of the dive brought momentary black-out, but when he could see clearly again the bomber appeared to be floating towards him, slowly, like a fish swimming lazily, so fast was he overtaking it. With cold deliberation he took it in the cross-lines of his sight, waited until he was well inside effective range, and then fired a long burst.

As the bullets struck the machine the enemy pilot turned flat at a speed that could have given his gunners no chance of returning the fire. Indeed, centrifugal force probably made it impossible for them to move at all. Biggles knew it, and seized the opportunity thus presented. Half rolling at the top of his zoom he brought his nose round and raked the bomber from airscrew to tailskid. The convulsive jerk of the machine told him that the pilot had been hit. For a moment it hung in the air, wallowing like a rolling porpoise, its airscrew clawing vainly at the super-heated atmosphere; then its nose swung down in a vicious stall which ended in a spin.

Biggles turned away from the stricken machine to meet the three Me. 109's that had followed in his wake. He had watched them in his reflector out of the tail of his eye. Behind them another machine was plunging earthward trailing smoke and flame. Another was gliding away. He could see only one Spitfire, but there was no time to look for the other. The three oncoming Me.'s, flying abreast, were launching a flank attack, and were already within five hundred feet, so he turned to take them head-on, firing at the same time. For a split second tracers flew between the Spitfire and the Messerschmitts. All four machines were shooting, and Biggles could feel bullets smashing through his wings. With his finger still on the firing button he held his machine steady and waited for the collision that seemed inevitable. He had no intention of turning away, for the first to turn away in head-on attack admits inferiority, and one of the first traditions laid down by the Flying Corps in the early days of air combat was 'never turn.'

At the last instant the Messerschmitts split and hurtled past on either side of him. Biggles was round with the speed of light. Choosing the centre machine, he clung to its tail, firing short bursts until a shadow falling across him made him kick out his foot and fling the joystick hard over. He was only just in time. A Messerschmitt flashed past, its tracer streaking through the spot where the Spitfire should have been but was not.

Biggles looked around, although one of the most difficult things in a dogfight is to keep in touch with events. A Messerschmitt with a Spitfire on its tail was racing towards the north. Three more Messerschmitts were scattered about the sky, converging on him—two of them from above, which he did not like. Still, he was not prepared to take the defensive, so, turning on the machine below him, he went down like a thunderbolt in a deliberate attempt to intimidate the pilot and so get him in a disadvantageous position before opening fire, for he knew he must be getting short of ammunition. He succeeded. The Messerschmitt dived, and in a desperate effort to escape the pilot pulled up and over in a terrific loop; but if by this means he hoped to throw the Spitfire off his tail he was doomed to disappointment. Biggles followed him into the loop, but at the top pulled the joystick into his stomach, so that his loop, instead of being a true circle, was cut to an oval. The Messerschmitt, completing its loop, was about to pass immediately below him. Biggles stood his machine on its nose and from a vertical position opened fire. The Messerschmitt flew straight into the stream of bullets.

Biggles had no time to watch the effect of his fire, for even while he was shooting he felt bullets hitting his own machine, and was obliged to roll out of the way. Looking round quickly for his assailant, he was just in time to see a Messerschmitt go to pieces in the air, some of the splinters narrowly missing another Me. that had evidently been keeping it company. Thoughts crowded into Biggles' brain, although to his racing nerves the scene seemed to be moving in slow motion. He wondered why the pilot of the broken machine, who was falling like a stone, did not use his parachute. He wondered what had caused the machine to disintegrate. A moment later he knew. An aircraft flashed across his nose. It was the Defiant, the gunner in the rear seat crouching over his gun. Angus had arrived.

Biggles took a deep breath, and looking around saw that the battle was over. A Spitfire was approaching from the north, gliding down to land. Two specks in the sky, fast disappearing, were all that remained of the Messerschmitts. Only he and the Defiant remained over the oasis, so after a last survey of the atmosphere he sideslipped down and landed. He was desperately anxious to know what had happened, for he had been too occupied to keep track of things. The Defiant followed him down.

One of the first things he saw as he jumped from his machine was Tex, limping in from the desert. There was a crimson streak on his left cheek, and one sleeve of his tunic hung in rags; but his face was wreathed in smiles.

'Suffering coyotes!' he cried deliriously. 'What a party!'

'Are you all right?' asked Biggles sharply.

'Sure I'm all right,' answered Tex cheerfully. 'More or less,' he added. 'I've lost a bit of skin here and there.'

'What about your machine?'

Tex pointed to a heap of wreckage that lay some way off, from the middle of which a crumpled tail stuck derisively into the air. 'She's finished, I guess. I got one guy, but his pal hit me with a ton of bricks and I lost a wing.'

Bertie taxied in and stood up in his cockpit, regarding Tex with disfavour through a glinting eyeglass. 'I say, look here, I wish you'd look where you're going. Really, you know, you jolly nearly scalped me,' he said severely.

144

The sight of a group of figures round the Defiant took Biggles to it at a run. A hush warned him of serious trouble, and a moment later he saw it. An air gunner, a corporal unknown to him, a fair lad with a boyish face, was being lifted carefully to the sand, where his head was pillowed on a parachute. His ashen face and a spreading crimson stain on the breast of his tunic told their own dire story. Angus, looking very upset, bent over him.

Biggles pushed his way to the front and dropped on his knees beside the wounded gunner. Looking up over his shoulder at Angus he said quietly: 'Who is it?'

'Boy from Wadi Halfa,' answered Angus in a broken voice. 'He volunteered to come with me. I thought I'd better have a gunner in case I ran into trouble. I wish now—'

'Wishing doesn't help anybody,' interrupted Biggles softly. 'You've nothing to reproach yourself with, Angus. These things will happen in a war, you know.'

He turned to the wounded man. Grey eyes looked into his own apologetically.

'Sorry, sir,' came in a faint whisper from the pallid lips.

'Sorry? What about?' asked Biggles.

'About giving you—this—trouble.'

'No need to worry about that,' replied Biggles gently. He had looked on similar scenes too often to deceive himself. He knew it was only a matter of minutes. There was nothing he could do—nothing anyone could do.

'I got—one,' whispered the dying gunner, with a twisted smile. 'He fired first—but I got—him.'

'Yes, you got him,' agreed Biggles—a fact which Angus confirmed.

145

Nobody else spoke.

'That's good enough—for me," breathed the airman. 'Wish I could have stayed—and seen—things through. I always wanted—to be—in your squadron—sir.'

'You're in it,' said Biggles, forcing a smile.

'Reckon I'm—booked—for topsides*—sir.'

'I reckon we all are,' answered Biggles grimly. 'It's just a matter of who goes first. Someone has to make a reconnaissance for the others.'

'That's right—sir.'

For a little while there was silence, while the sun sank behind the oasis in a sea of gold, causing the palms to throw out long shadows like arms towards the little group. The boy muttered once or twice as his mind wandered, while the light faded from his eyes, serenely, as it faded from the sky. Then with a little sigh his head dropped into Biggles' arms.

Biggles laid the head gently on the parachute and stood up.

'That's all,' he said.

'I shouldn't ha' brought the lad,' blurted Angus.

'Forget it,' Biggles told him calmly. 'This is war, not kindergarten. To-day it was the boy's bad luck. To-morrow it may be me—or you. You know that. He didn't bleat about it. Neither, I hope, shall we, when our turn comes.' He turned to the flight-sergeant. 'All right,' he said in a normal voice. 'Carry him in. We'll bury him to-night. All ranks will attend. By the way, what happened to the bomber?'

'Went into the ground with the engine full on, sir. Everyone in it must have been killed.'

Biggles nodded. 'Better bring in the enemy casualties.

---

* Slang: heaven.

146

They can be buried at the same time. I want all officers in the mess tent, please. We'll have a check up. You'd better come along, too, Flight-Sergeant, when you've given your orders.'

Through the quickly-fading twilight, Biggles, with the others following, led the way to the tent.

Chapter 13
Biggles Takes His Turn

When they were inside the tent Tex was the first to speak. 'How about von Zoyton?' he asked. 'Was he among the people we shot down?'

'No,' answered Biggles, shortly.

'How do you know that?'

'Because I fancy that had von Zoyton been over some of us might not now be here. I've seen him fly, and there was nothing like his tactics in this evening's affair. You'll find he didn't come. He was probably exhausted after his night in the desert. He'll be over soon, though, now he knows how short we are of machines.'

'How can he know we are short?' demanded Bertie.

'Because we only put up three Spitfires against seven hostile machines this afternoon. Von Zoyton isn't a fool. Obviously, he will know perfectly well that if we had had more we should have used them.'

'Of course—absolutely—I didn't think of that,' muttered Bertie. 'Good thing you're here to do the thinking.'

Biggles pulled out a camp chair. 'Sit down, everybody, and we'll see how things look. I still don't know exactly how the show finished. All I know is we're down to two Spitfires, and they both need patching—at least, mine does. The tail looks like a sieve. Von Zoyton can't have many machines left, either. He'll have still fewer, I hope, when we've had our innings.'

The check-up, to which the flight sergeant largely contributed, for he had watched the whole thing from the ground, revealed that the battle had been won at really very small cost. They had lost only one man killed, the volunteer gunner of the Defiant. Tex had been slightly hurt. A cannon shell had exploded in his cockpit tearing a nasty gash in his face; he had also wrenched the muscles of a leg when landing by parachute. His machine was destroyed. The two other Spitfires had been damaged, but both were serviceable. On the German side the bomber had been destroyed and its three occupants killed. Three Messerschmitt 109's had also been destroyed for certain, all the pilots being killed. One, apparently, had baled out, but his parachute had not opened. Another 109, the one that had been chased by Bertie, had been damaged, and might not have reached its base. Bertie had abandoned the pursuit when he had run out of ammunition. The two remaining Messerschmitts had presumably got home. If von Zoyton had come on the show he must have been in one of these, for his body was not among the Nazi dead; Biggles was convinced, however, that he had not been with the attacking formation.

'It comes to this,' he said, at the end of the summing up. 'We're down to the two Spitfires and the Defiant. Von Zoyton has lost more than we have, but he started with more; at this moment he must be short of machines—unless, of course, he is in a position to call up reinforcements. He won't hesitate to do that if he can get some. One of the outstanding Nazi characteristics is vanity, and it would be gall and wormwood for him to have to admit that we got the better of him. He'll do anything rather than allow that to happen.'

'What are you going to do about it?' asked Algy.

'Two Spitfires and a Defiant isn't much of a striking force.'

'You're right; it isn't. I'd like to get the four Spits that are at Karga over here right away, but I'm not clear as to how it can be done.'

'We could use the Defiant to take people to Karga—'

'Yes, I know,' interrupted Biggles, 'but I wanted the Defiant for another purpose. You see, even if we got the four Spitfires here it wouldn't prevent the Nazis from putting up their magnetic disturbance in the morning and throwing the air liner off its course. As a matter of fact, I had formed a plan when the Nazis came over this afternoon, and I feel inclined to go on with it.' Biggles lit a cigarette before continuing.

'This is my idea. The scheme has for its first objective the destruction of the Nazi electrical equipment. If we can do that we not only put an end to this compass juggling, but we silence von Zoyton's radio. If that part of the programme was successful, and conditions were favourable, I should strike right away at a second objective. As I told you, the Nazis are holding a Rapide which they forced down intact while it was flying over the route. I should try to get the Rapide, and collecting the prisoners at the same time bring them home in it. That would not only remove the handicap which prevents us from shooting up von Zoyton's base, but would provide us with a transport machine which we need badly. Then, with the prisoners out of the way, and the Karga Spitfires here, we could keep Wadi Umbo on the jump, and at the same time keep the air clear over the route. Make no mistake, as things stand, now von Zoyton knows where we are, Salima is going to be anything but a health resort. I'm sorry to be so

150

long-winded about all this, but I always try to ensure that everyone knows how things are going. Now we know what we want, let us consider ways and means of putting it over.

'We can't shoot up the Nazis for reasons which I have already explained. That means the job has to be done on the ground. I propose to do it myself, not because I don't think any of you could do it, but because I know just where the lorries are parked. This is the programme as I've mapped it out in my mind. If anyone sees a weak spot, say so. Zero hour will be twelve midnight. At eleven o'clock Algy will fly the Defiant to a point near Wadi Umbo where Ginger and I will bale out. Algy will then return home. At twelve midnight the show will open with Bertie and Tug, in the two Spitfires, shooting up Wadi Umbo aerodrome but keeping away from the southern end of the oasis to avoid hitting the prisoners. They will make as much noise as possible. Under cover of the confusion that should result from this effort, Ginger and I will slip into the oasis. I shall tackle the lorries. Ginger will go to the Rapide and get ready to start up when I arrive. If I see a chance I shall collect the prisoners before joining Ginger in the Rapide, which will take off and fly to Salima. When the two Spitfires see the Rapide take off they also will return home. The Rapide will land here, and as soon as convenient fly on to Karga, taking four pilots to bring back the Spitfires. That's a broad outline of the scheme. Of course, it has one weak point. If Ginger and I can't get the Rapide we shan't be able to fly home, but as far as I can see there's no alternative. We daren't risk a night landing in the Defiant, in unknown country, with rock all over the place. The Nazis have cleared an area for an aerodrome, but we could hardly use that. Any questions?'

'But what about the rest of us, look you?' cried Taffy, in a pained voice. 'Don't we get in the game whatsoever?'

'Angus can't come because he'll have to remain in charge here. Someone will have to stay, and I say Angus because he had been in the air most of the day and must be dead beat. Tex, with a wounded head and a game leg, is in no condition to fly.'

'That still leaves me, Ferocity and Henry,' Taffy pointed out. 'Can't we do something useful?'

'You can form three of the party to go to Karga in the Rapide to fetch the Spitfires,' suggested Biggles.

'We could do that anyway,' complained Taffy. 'I was thinking about the big show.'

'All right. I'll tell you what you can do,' offered Biggles. 'Walk to the armoured car, taking a working party, and dig it out. If you can't get it out, or if the engine is dud, you'll have a nice stroll home again in the moonlight. If it's all right you can patrol between here and Wadi Umbo in case anyone has to make a forced landing. If you start right away you should have the car clear before midnight.'

'I seem to do nothing but chase round the landscape in that perishing battle-wagon,' growled Taffy.

'I can't give you an aircraft because I haven't any,' Biggles pointed out. Then he smiled. 'After all, you left your Spitfire at Karga when you came here—without orders. Had you remained at your station I could now have sent you a signal to fly over and join in the fun and games.'

'All right, sir, you win,' agreed Taffy. 'Come on,

Henry; come on, Ferocity! Let's go and examine von Zoyton's tin chariot.'

'If we can get the four Spitfires here by morning we'll give von Zoyton the shock of his life if, as I think, he's worked it out that we're down to two machines,' declared Biggles. 'Now let's synchronise our watches and polish up the details of the scheme. In a show like this perfect timing is essential.'

With the scheme afoot the time passed quickly. The melancholy business of the funerals took up a certain amount of time, as did the evening meal, and it was after ten before all these things had been cleared up. Taffy, Ferocity and Henry, with spades on their shoulders, had long ago set off for the abandoned car. In the end they had decided to do the work themselves rather than take from the oasis airmen who were working full time on the two Spitfires, both of which needed attention.

Silence utter and complete lay over the desert when, just before eleven, the operating machines were wheeled out to the open sand in readiness for the raid. The great African moon gleamed like polished silver in a cloudless sky. The palms of the oasis, weary after their battle with the sun, hung silently at rest.

'It's going to be a bit of a squash, I'm afraid,' remarked Biggles to Ginger, as they walked over to the Defiant.

'We'll get in somehow,' said Ginger.

'When we bale out, follow me down as quickly as you can,' went on Biggles. 'We don't want to land too far apart.'

'How do you want me to fly?' inquired Algy.

'Take her up to twenty thousand. Cut your engine and glide when I give the word. We want to get as close as we can, but it won't do for the enemy to hear us. When we've baled out, turn and glide away; try not to use your engine until you are out of earshot of the aerodrome.'

Algy nodded. 'Okay. I get it.'

Biggles finished his cigarette and stamped the stub into the sand. He looked at his watch. 'All right,' he said, 'let's be going.'

Algy climbed into his seat. Biggles and Ginger followed, and wedged themselves in the gunner's cockpit—the gun had been removed to make more room.

The engine came to life, shattering the silence and swirling sand in little clouds across the desert. The aircraft began to move forward, slowly at first but with swiftly increasing speed. The tail lifted. Then the Defiant rose with the grace of a bird towards the dome of heaven. Picking up its course it continued to nose its way upward, without effort, each succeeding thousand feet of height thrusting the horizon ever farther away. At first the sand had glistened faintly to the stars, but from fifteen thousand feet the aircraft appeared scarcely to move across a bowl of immense size, the interior of which was as dull and lifeless as the surface of the moon. Indeed, the picture presented reminded Ginger of those he had seen of the moon, photographed through a telescopic lens. Oases were represented by dark spots that might have been no more than clumps of moss. All detail was lost. The only landmark was the ancient slave trail which, as straight as a railway track, crept up over the rim of the world to cut a tragic scar across its face before disappearing into the mysterious shadows that veiled the northern horizon. And still the aircraft thrust its way towards stars that seemed to hang like fairy lamps from a ceiling of purple velvet.

Biggles spoke to Algy. 'Level out and cut the engine,' he ordered. 'There's Wadi Umbo ahead. Five minutes will do it.'

As the nose came down the drone of the engine died away to a sibilant whisper. The aircraft glided on through a lonely sky, leaving no more sign of its passing than a fish in deep water. Biggles, his face expressionless, watched the ground. The minutes passed slowly, as they always do in the air. But at last he turned to Ginger.

'Let's go,' he said. 'Give me three seconds to get clear. We should be able to see each other when we get on the floor.' To Algy he said, 'So long—see you later.'

Algy nodded. He did not speak.

Biggles climbed out, slid a little way along the fuselage, and then dropped off into space.

Ginger could see him falling like a stone as he climbed on the fuselage and followed his leader into the void. The experience was no novelty, and as soon as his parachute had opened he looked around calmly to make out what appeared to be a mushroom, a thousand feet below and about a quarter of a mile behind in the track of the aircraft. After that there was nothing more to do but wait while the brolly lowered him gently through the atmosphere.

There was no wind, so he knew that he was dropping vertically. Not that there was any sensation of falling. He appeared to be suspended in space. In fact, he was not conscious of any sensation at all, except perhaps one of loneliness. He appeared to be alone in the world. The silence was uncanny. It was some time before the details of the desert, such as they were, began to draw nearer and take shape. As far as he could make out he would touch down, as was intended, between two and three miles short of the objective, the oasis that lay like a dark stain on a grey cloth.

Then, suddenly, came a feeling of falling, for no other reason than because the earth seemed to rise swiftly to meet him, and he bent his knees to take the shock of landing. He watched the ground with some apprehension, for he knew that if he struck rock instead of sand it might mean a broken bone. But as it happened all was well, and he landed on the sand as gently as he could ever remember alighting. He did not even fall. The silk, as soon as his weight was taken from it, settled as softly as a thistle seed. In a moment he was out of his harness, rolling the fabric into a loose ball. This done, knowing the direction, he gazed across the desert, and was relieved to see a figure walking towards him. Biggles had, of course, landed first.

'What are we going to do with the brollies?' asked Ginger, when they met. 'We can't hump them round with us; they'll be in the way.'

'We shall have to abandon them,' answered Biggles, in a low voice. He walked a little way to the nearest rock. 'We'll cover them with sand, and smooth it out,' he said. 'We may have a chance to recover them at some future date.' As he spoke Biggles set down a bundle that he was carrying and started to scoop a hole in the sand.

It took about ten minutes to dispose of the unwanted parachutes. Then Biggles rose, picking up his parcel.

'Now let's get along,' he said. 'We've some way to go, but we've plenty of time. We'll keep close to the rock. I hope we shan't see anybody, and I don't think we shall, but if we're challenged we may have to fight it out. Got your gun handy?'

'I brought two, to be on the safe side,' answered Ginger.

Biggles smiled. 'Not a bad idea. I hope it won't come to that, though. But that's enough talking. Don't speak unless you have something important to say; it's amazing how far sound travels when the desert is as quiet as this.'

Biggles took a small service compass from his pocket, studied it for a moment and then walked on, keeping close against an outcrop of rock that ran like the carapace on a crocodile's back in the right direction.

Chapter 14
The Storm Breaks

For half an hour Biggles walked on, keeping close against the rock and stopping often to listen. Occasionally he made a cautious survey of the country ahead from the top of a convenient eminence, taking care, though, not to show too much of himself above the skyline. Ginger did not speak, for he had nothing to say. In the end it was Biggles who, after a reconnaissance, broke the long silence.

'We're about three hundred yards from the fringe of the oasis,' he breathed. 'The camel lines are to our left. I can see people moving about, but I think we can risk getting a little closer. We're in good time.'

'What is the time?' whispered Ginger.

'A quarter to twelve.'

They went on again, slowly, exercising extreme caution, and after a little while came to a cup-shaped depression in the rocks. Sounds of movement, industry, and noisy conversation in the oasis were now clearly audible.

'This will do us,' announced Biggles. 'We'll stay here till the music starts.'

Ginger squatted down to wait. 'Everything seems to be going fine,' he observed.

Biggles shrugged his shoulders. 'You can never tell. However well a show like this is planned, much still depends on sheer chance. One can't make allowances for the unexpected, for things one doesn't know about.

I should say that good leadership consists not so much of sitting down quietly at a headquarters and making plans, as adapting them to meet unexpected obstacles as they occur. Everything is all right so far. We'll deal with trouble when it arises—as it probably will. We shall be lucky if it doesn't. We're all set. There are still ten minutes to go.'

'Sounds like the lads coming now,' murmured Ginger a moment later, as the distant hum of aircraft came rolling through the night air.

Biggles said nothing for a little while. 'That doesn't sound like a pair of Spitfires to me. The sound is coming from the wrong direction, anyway.'

It was now Ginger's turn to be silent. Standing up he gazed long and steadily towards the north, the direction from which the sound seemed to come. Presently there was no doubt about it. 'There are more than two engines there,' he announced.

'More than two!' retorted Biggles. 'I should say there are nearer ten. They're not our engines. To me, that broken purr says Junkers*. They're coming this way— they must be coming here. We've chosen a lovely time for a raid!' He looked over the rim of the depression. 'Everyone seems to be making for the aerodrome,' he remarked. 'We'd better get a bit nearer and see what is happening. Junkers or not, those lorries have got to be destroyed, somehow. Come on!'

Sometimes walking and sometimes running they made their way quickly towards the oasis. If they were seen there was no indication of it. There was a considerable amount of noise, suggesting excitement, in the

* JU52—German three-engined, low-wing monoplane used for transporting many passengers.

enemy camp. Orders were shouted. The drone of aircraft became a roar. There was no longer any need to talk quietly. Landing lights sprang up round the aerodrome, and a floodlight flung a path of radiance across it.

Biggles made swiftly for the fringe of palms that marked the nearest point of the oasis. Reaching it, he hesitated. Anxious as he was to get to the lorries, he was equally concerned about the landing aircraft, for he could not imagine what they could be or what they were doing. He glanced at his watch.

'Four minutes to go,' he said crisply. 'I think we've time to see what all this fuss is about.'

They hurried forward through the palms until they reached a position which gave them a view of the enemy landing ground. As they came within sight of it a big machine was just coming in.

'For the love of Mike!' ejaculated Biggles. 'It's an old Junkers commercial, the type Lufthansa* used on the Berlin-Croydon run. What the . . .' Biggles' voice faded away in speechless astonishment as one after another four of the big tri-motored machines landed, filling the air with noise and turbulent sand. But an even greater shock was to come. As the machines came to a standstill cabin doors were opened and men poured out to form up with military precision. Not fewer than twenty men in full marching order emerged from each of the first three machines.

'Paratroops,' said Biggles in a curiously calm voice.

'What on earth would they want with paratroops in this part of the world?' demanded Ginger in astonishment.

---

* German state airline

Biggles threw him a sidelong glance. 'I'll give you one guess,' he said.

'You mean—Salima?'

'What else? This is von Zoyton's answer. He must have sent for them from North Africa.'

The big machines now moved forward, like four antediluvian monsters, making for a part of the oasis not far from where Biggles and Ginger stood watching. Three rumbled on and disappeared between the palms. The last one stopped. Men ran out and swarmed about it.

'Now what?' said Ginger.

The question was soon answered. Six anti-aircraft guns of the pom-pom type were quickly unloaded.

'I imagine those are intended as a little surprise in case we come over,' said Biggles grimly. 'Oh to be in the air at this moment with a full load of ammunition.'

'What a target for Bertie and Tug when they come over!'

Biggles looked at his watch. 'They'll be thirty seconds too late,' he said bitterly. 'There's still half a minute to go. There goes the last of the Junkers into the trees. Now the lights are going out. It's all over.'

'But Bertie and Tug will have seen something going on. They can't be far away.'

'Probably, but they won't know what to make of it. In any case, they have their orders.' Biggles bit his lip with annoyance. 'This is the sort of thing that tempts one to depart from the original plan, but we mustn't do that,' he muttered. 'We must go through with what we started. Hark! Here come the Spitfires now. Everyone will be busy with the new arrivals, so we still have a chance. This way.' Biggles began walking quickly through the palms towards the centre of the oasis. There were quite a number of troops about, and one

161

or two passed fairly close, but no one challenged the intruders.

Two minutes sharp walk brought them to a clearing, and by this time pandemonium had broken loose. Such was the uproar that Ginger, after the first shock of astonishment had passed, in spite of the seriousness of their position, burst out laughing. Rising above everything was the howl of the Spitfires, which were literally skimming the palm fronds at the bottom of each dive. Occasionally they used their guns, filling the air with streams of tracer shells and bullets. All sorts of weapons came into action on the ground. Musketry rolled. Orders were screamed. Men ran, shouting, apparently under the impression that the oasis was being attacked by a superior force. A pom-pom gun, presumably one of the new ones, added its voice to the din.

'Strewth!' muttered Biggles, 'what a business.' He caught Ginger by the arm and pointed. 'Look! There's the Rapide. Now's your chance. Get set, but don't start up until I join you.'

As Ginger made a bee-line for the big machine, Biggles, revolver in one hand and parcel under the other arm, darted along the edge of the clearing to where he had last seen the lorries. His satisfaction was intense when he saw they were still there. He ran forward until he was close enough to hear a dynamo whirring.

Suddenly a man, armed with a rifle, bayonet fixed, appeared in front of him. Whether he was a sentry, or merely an odd soldier on his way to the landing ground. Biggles never knew. At first the man took no notice of him, but, unfortunately, as they were about to pass, a star-shell cut a brilliant parabola across the sky, and showed everything in clear white light. Had the man gone on Biggles would have taken no notice of him, for he was concerned only with the destruction of the lorries; but it seemed that the soldier suddenly recognized Biggles' uniform. At any rate, he pulled up dead and shouted, '*Wie gehts da*?*' At the same time he dropped the point of his bayonet, ready to thrust.

With a swift movement of his free arm Biggles knocked the muzzle of the rifle aside. The cartridge exploded. The blaze nearly blinded him. Before he had fully recovered his sight the man had jumped forward and knocked him over backwards. Biggles fired as he fell, and the man slipped forward like a swimmer diving into deep water. Picking himself up, Biggles looked around quickly, hoping that in the general uproar the shots would not have been noticed. But apparently they had, for a door in the rear of the nearest lorry, which was built in the manner of a caravan, was flung open, so that light streamed out. In the centre of it, peering forward, stood a German airman. He was hatless and his tunic was unfastened, suggesting that he was either an engineer or radio operator. In his hand he held a revolver.

Things were not going quite as smoothly as Biggles had hoped, but there could be no question of retiring. The man saw him and shouted something, and without waiting for a reply fired two quick shots, neither of which hit their mark. Biggles took quick but deliberate aim and fired. The man stumbled out of the lorry on to the sand, ran a few yards, and fell. Biggles took no further notice of him, but jumped into the lorry to find it empty.

As he had supposed, the interior was a compact, perfectly equipped radio station. He unwrapped his parcel. It was not, as Ginger had vaguely supposed, a

* German: Who goes there?

bomb, or an explosive charge, for the simple reason that nothing of the sort was available at Salima. Biggles had been compelled to rely on fire alone, and he carried in his parcel no more than a large oil can filled with petrol.

It took him only a moment to remove the cap and splash the contents over the walls and floors of the lorry. He backed to the door, laying a trail of spirit, for he had no intention of being burnt when the petrol gas exploded, as he knew it would when he applied a light. The second lorry stood so close to the first that the destruction of one would be bound to involve the other. Nevertheless, he flung what remained of the petrol on the nearest wall of it, and then, having struck a match, tossed it on the petrol-soaked sand. There was a sheet of blue fire, a vicious *whoosh*, and the first lorry was immediately enveloped in flame. Blue flame dripped from the adjacent vehicle.

Biggles backed away, watching to make sure that his work had been well done. A minute sufficed to convince him that it had, so he turned and ran towards the prison hut. What was going on in other parts of the oasis he did not know, but the commotion neither in the air nor on the ground had in any way subsided, and that was all he cared.

When he reached the long hutment that housed the prisoners he found a curious state of affairs. It appeared that the prisoners, alarmed or excited by the uproar, had crowded outside the hut to see what was going on. As they were not tied up this was possible, although in the ordinary way they would have been intimated by the sentries, who were always on duty. The sentries were, in fact, still there, two of them, brandishing their rifles and shouting in an attempt to drive the prisoners back into their quarters. When Biggles arrived on the scene, the prisoners, talking excitedly, were just moving back into the hut, although they still tried to see what was going on, hoping, no doubt, that British troops had arrived to rescue them.

One of the sentries saw Biggles coming at a run, shouted something, and levelled his rifle. Biggles swerved and the bullet whizzed harmlessly past him. Before the man could fire again, Biggles' gun had spat, and the man fell. The other sentry turned and ran, shouting for help. Biggles stopped and addressed the prisoners tersely.

'Keep your heads,' he said. 'I'm trying to get you away. Stay together and follow me.'

'Well, strike Old Harry!' cried a voice. 'Isn't that Biggles?'

Biggles stared at the speaker and recognized Freddie Gillson, the Imperial Airways captain of whom he had spoken, and who he had often met at Croydon.

'Hello, Fred,' he said. 'You're the very man I want. Can you handle a Rapide?'

'I should think so,' replied Fred, grinning. 'I brought one here—that's my machine they've got.'

'Fine! We're going home in it—I hope,' snapped Biggles. 'Keep close to me. Make for the cockpit as soon as we reach the machine. A lad of mine is inside, but he may not know for certain how everything works. You take over. Come on.'

Biggles turned and ran towards the Rapide, which he could not see, although he knew that it was only a hundred yards or so away.

The prisoners followed, and it looked as though they would reach their objective unmolested. But this was not to be, for, although Biggles was not to know it, the

165

aircraft stood in full view of a spot which had been manned by German paratroops who were lining the fringe of the palms overlooking the landing ground in order to resist the attack which they supposed was being launched. Even then the escapers nearly succeeded in getting aboard without being noticed, for it seemed that the Nazis were concerned only with what was in front of them. Fred had already entered the Rapide, and the others were crowding in behind him when, by a bit of bad luck, one of the German soldiers happened to look round. Even then, possibly because he was a new arrival, he appeared not to understand exactly what was going on. For a moment he just gazed without any particular interest. Then he seemed to realise that something was wrong. He ran a few paces towards the Rapide and then stopped, staring, evidently trying to make out just what was happening. Suddenly he understood and let out a yell.

'Inside everybody—quick!' shouted Biggles. 'I'll keep them back. Don't wait for me. Get off as fast as you can.'

So saying, Biggles ran a little way towards the end of the line of German troops, who by this time had turned towards the scene, and dropping into a fold in the sand opened fire with his revolver. He reckoned that another minute would see all the escapers in the aircraft, and his action was calculated to gain just that amount of time. And in this he was successful. Before his fire, the Germans, thrown into some confusion by so unexpectedly finding themselves enfiladed*, ducked for fresh cover, and by the time they were in a position to do anything the Rapide's engines had come to life;

* Enfilade: To attack a line of troops or targets by firing from the side down its length.

166

the big machine began to move slowly towards the open ground, its airscrews flinging dust and palm debris high into the air.

This was the moment for which Biggles had waited. There was no longer any point in remaining, for it was not his intention to be left behind. Jumping to his feet he made a dash for the cabin door, which had been left open. Several shots were fired at him, as he knew they would be, but there was no way of preventing this. The Rapide turned a little, presumably to help him, but the result was a blinding cloud of dust right in his face. Instinctively he flung up an arm to protect his eyes. At that moment a rifle cracked, but he did not hear it. Something inside his head seemed to explode in a sheet of crimson flame that faded slowly to utter blackness. He pitched forward on his face and lay still.

Chapter 15

Abandoned

Probably only one man of all those in the vicinity saw
Biggles fall—Ginger, who from the cockpit had seen
his perilous position, and had dashed to the door to
cover his retreat. Biggles, as he fell, was hidden from
the Germans by the clouds of dust torn up by the
churning airscrews. In the general rush, those in the
machine were too concerned with their own affairs to
look outside. What had happened was this.

Ginger had found the Rapide and reached it with
surprising ease. Germans were all around him, but not
one took the slightest notice of him, this being due, no
doubt, to the uproar, which at its worst appeared to
produce a state of panic. Entering the cockpit he made
a quick survey of the instruments and then proceeded
to put the machine in a condition for a quick start-
up and take-off. This occupied him for some minutes,
during which time he was left quite alone, although
there was nothing remarkable about this. There was
no reason why the Germans should suppose anyone
was in the air liner. This done, he was able to turn his
attention to what was going on outside. The dominant
feature was a fire of sufficient size to throw a lurid glow
over everything. Through the dancing shadows of the
palms, cast by the leaping flames, he could see figures
moving, most in ones and twos. There was as yet no
sign of Biggles, who, he realised with a glow of satisfac-

tion, had succeeded in his first object—the destruction of the Nazi power station.

After two or three minutes had elapsed he saw, not without consternation, that German paratroops were lining the edge of the oasis uncomfortably close to his position; but there was nothing he could do about it. Shortly afterwards he made out a little crowd running towards the Rapide, and knew that Biggles had managed to secure the prisoners. Two figures, running hard, were in advance of the main group.

What happened next has already been related. One of the two leading figures, whom he now perceived was Biggles, turned towards the paratroops. The other ran on and jumped into the machine. This man was a stranger to Ginger, but he introduced himself without wasting words.

'I'm Gillson,' he rapped out. 'This is my machine. Let me have her. Where are we bound for?'

'Salima—an oasis about a hundred and thirty miles south-east from here. You can see it for miles—you can't miss it.'

'Okay,' returned Gillson shortly. 'You'd better go and look after your C.O. He's outside somewhere.'

Looking through the side window, Ginger saw how dangerously Biggles was placed. He was content to leave the aircraft in the hands of a master pilot, so he made his way to the cabin door, where he found the rest of the prisoners pouring in. This prevented him from getting out. All he could do was to shout, 'Hurry along—hurry along,' in the manner of a bus conductor.

The prisoners did not need the invitation. They were only too anxious to get aboard, but for several seconds they prevented Ginger from seeing what was going on outside. He could, however, hear the crack of rifle fire, which worried him. When finally the door was clear, he looked out to see Biggles retiring towards the Rapide in a cloud of dust. Then the machine began to move. This alarmed Ginger, although as the movement was as yet slight he hoped that Biggles would manage to get on board. More sand swirled, half hiding the scene.

By this time Ginger was shooting at the Germans as fast as he could pull trigger. He did not trouble to take aim, but blazed away simply with the idea of keeping up a hot covering fire. Then Biggles, when he was within a dozen yards of the aircraft, pitched headlong on the sand. For a moment Ginger did nothing, for his first impression was that Biggles had merely fallen; but when he did not get up he realised with a shock that he had been hit. At this juncture the aircraft turned still more towards the landing ground, driving a blinding cloud of dust straight into the faces of the Germans. The scene was completely blotted out. Ginger could no longer see Biggles although he was only a few yards away. He did what anyone would have done in the circumstances. He jumped out of the machine and, running to the place where he had last seen him, found him still lying as he had fallen.

With the object of carrying him to the aircraft, Ginger tried to pick him up, only to discover that to pick up an unconscious body is not the simple job some people may suppose. It is far more difficult than picking up a man who is only pretending to be unconscious. In sheer desperation he seized Biggles by the collar and started to drag him. He could hear the machine, but he could not see it on account of the flying sand which, flung into his face with considerable force, nearly blinded him. For a minute he struggled on in a kind of frenzy. He knew it was no use shouting for help because the roar of the Rapide's engines drowned all other sounds. Then, to his horror, the sound began to recede, and as the aircraft gathered speed such a storm of wind and sand and debris was hurled behind it that Ginger dropped choking to his knees, covering his face with his arms.

As soon as it was reasonably possible he stood up. He knew that he had been left behind, and for a little while the shock bereft him of all power of thought. His brain whirled as a thousand thoughts crowded into it. Biggles still lay at his feet, dead or wounded, he did not know which. Overhead, the noise of aircraft began to abate, and he could hear orders being shouted through the settling sand, which was still dense enough to prevent him from seeing more than a few yards. Not knowing what he was going to do—in fact, hardly knowing what he was doing—he grasped Biggles by the collar of his tunic and started to drag him in the direction of the nearest palms. He knew where they were. Reaching them he halted, and tried to think.

He was now out of the line of the Rapide's take-off, and the air was comparatively clear. There was still a certain amount of noise, mostly in the direction of the burning lorries. Judging by sounds, everyone on the oasis was there, trying to extinguish the flames. Overhead the moon shone brightly, throwing a complicated pattern of shadows on the sand.

Ginger dropped on his knees and looked at Biggles in the hope of discovering where he had been hit. This was not difficult, for his face was covered with blood. With his handkerchief he was able to wipe most of it away, revealing a wound just above Biggles' right ear. As far as he could make out it was a long laceration, tearing away skin and hair. Another fraction of an inch and the bullet would have missed him altogether; a fraction the other way and it would have gone right through his head.

Ginger decided that there was only one thing to do. He was not in the least concerned with being taken prisoner; he was concerned only in saving Biggles' life, if possible. The Germans, being in force, would have a medical officer with them. Clearly he must give himself up in order to get assistance. Before doing this, however, he soaked his handkerchief with water from the water bottle which he carried, and dabbed it on Biggles' face. He also tried to pour a little through the pallid lips.

Unexpectedly, and to his joy, Biggles groaned, muttered incoherently for a moment and then opened his eyes. They stared at Ginger unseeingly.

Recklessly, Ginger poured more water on Biggles' head, and was overjoyed to see his eyes clear.

'What happened?' whispered Biggles in a weak voice.

'You've been hit,' answered Ginger. 'We're still at Wadi Umbo. The Rapide got away with the prisoners, but we were left behind.'

Biggles struggled to a sitting position, drank from the water bottle, and then buried his face in his hands. Presently he looked up. 'We seem to be in a mess,' he muttered. 'My head's thumping like a steam hammer.'

'I'm going to fetch a doctor,' declared Ginger.

'No!' Biggles' voice was firm. 'Don't do that. I don't think it's as bad as that. I'm still a bit dizzy, but maybe I'll be better presently. I'll give it a minute or two, anyway.' Biggles laved his hands and face with water, while Ginger took the field service dressing from the corner of his tunic* and bandaged Biggles' head.

'That's better already,' announced Biggles. 'By gosh! That was a close one, though. Where exactly are we?'

Ginger told him.

'Where are the Germans?'

'I think they're trying to put out the fire. I can't make out why they haven't found us.'

'Probably because they haven't looked,' murmured Biggles. 'Naturally, they would assume we had got away in the Rapide.'

'Of course—I didn't think of that.'

Biggles rose unsteadily to his feet and stood swaying. He leaned against a palm to steady himself. 'I don't feel like packing up—yet,' he said. 'We've got a chance. Let's try to find a better position. The best place, if we can get to it, is the side of the oasis where we came in. The palms are pretty thick there, and I don't think it's used much.'

'Okay, if you think you can manage it,' agreed Ginger. 'You'd better put your arm round my shoulders. I'll help to steady you.'

Then began a long slow walk as they worked their way cautiously towards the desired position. Biggles' condition improved, partly, no doubt, as the result of his iron constitution, and partly on account of his will power. Comparative quiet had fallen on the oasis. An argument appeared to be going on at the place where the lorries had stood. A glow marked the spot. Occasionally figures could be seen moving through the trees. Eventually the objective was reached, and there,

---

* Every serviceman carried a wound dressing kit for emergency first aid.

just inside the palms, facing the open sand, Biggles sat down to rest.

'How are you feeling?' asked Ginger anxiously.

'Not too bad,' returned Biggles. 'I've got a splitting skull ache, otherwise I seem to be all right.'

'How about trying to pinch a Messerschmitt?' suggested Ginger.

Biggles smiled bleakly. 'I don't think I'm quite up to that. Let's sit quietly for a bit and think things over. Everything went off fine. It's just a matter of getting home, now.'

As they sat and rested, every now and then, from somewhere in the desert, voices could be heard, calling. For some time they took no notice. Then Biggles looked up.

'What the deuce is going on out there?' he asked.

Ginger moved a little nearer to the open sand and gazed out across the wilderness. He could just make out several figures, apparently walking aimlessly, some near, some far. One or two were leading camels.

'I get it,' he said slowly. 'The Spitfires, or the general commotion, must have stampeded the camels. They're all over the place, and the Arabs are out looking for them.'

'Is that so?' said Biggles, in an interested voice. 'Are there any camels in the camel lines—you know, the Toureg camp?'

'Yes, several.'

'See any Arabs?'

Ginger looked long and carefully. 'No. They all seem to be out looking for the strays. Those who bring them back just tie them up and then go out to look for more.'

Said Biggles, in a curious voice: 'Ginger, have you ever ridden on a camel?'

'Come to think of it, I don't think I have,' answered Ginger. 'Why?'

'Because,' returned Biggles, 'I'm afraid you are going to have a perfectly beastly time.'

Ginger started. 'Doing what?'

'Having your first lesson.'

'What's wrong with a camel?'

'Quite a lot of things,' murmured Biggles. 'To start with, he is usually as bad-tempered as he is ugly. His breath stinks like nothing on earth, and if he doesn't like you he may spit in your eye a slimy lump of green cud. Riding a camel is like sitting on a broomstick in a choppy sea.'

'Why are you telling me this?' inquired Ginger, in a startled voice.

'Because this seems to be where we go riding on a camel in the desert—or rather, on two camels.'

Biggles got to his feet and surveyed the camel lines, which were quite near. 'I think it's all clear,' he observed. 'Let's go across. I'm no lover of a camel, but I'd rather use his feet than mine, when it comes to foot work on the sand.'

Five camels stood in the line, contentedly chewing the cud. Three carried saddles; two were unsaddled. Biggles went up to the nearest beast that carried a saddle.

'You will discover that a camel saddle is designed primarily for breaking your back,' he observed. 'The first thing, though, is to make the animal kneel, so you can get on his back.' Then, looking at the camel, he said, '*Ikh*.'

The animal took no notice.

'I hope I haven't lost the knack,' muttered Biggles.

'You have to get just the right intonation.' He tried again, with a more guttural accent. '*Ikh.*'

The animal groaned, and sank on its knees.

'There you are—all done by kindness,' Biggles told Ginger. 'Get aboard. Sit side-saddle on the rug. Get the pommel in the bend of your right leg and hook your instep with your left heel. That's the idea. Hold tight!' Then, to the camel, he said, '*Dhai*!'

Ginger grabbed at his saddle as an earthquake occurred under the front half of his camel, tilting him back at an angle of forty-five degrees. He leaned forward to prevent himself from sliding off; simultaneously the rear half of the camel heaved, and he was restored to even keel. He caught his breath when he looked down and saw how far he was from the ground.

Meanwhile Biggles had followed the same procedure with a second camel. Mounted, he drew near to Ginger. 'You can hold your rein—there's only one—but it doesn't really do anything. You guide a camel by tapping its neck and regulate your speed with your heel. No doubt your beast will follow mine.' To his camel Biggles said, '*Yahh!*', and the beast started to walk.

Ginger found himself lurching backwards and forwards, just as though, as Biggles had said, he was on a rough sea.

'I shan't be able to stand much of this,' he muttered. 'I shall be as sick as a dog.'

'That's all right,' Biggles assured him. 'You'll find it a bit tricky when we break into a trot; but if you can hang on while the beast gets in its stride, you'll find a camel easier to ride than a horse—look out! Those two fellows on the right have spotted us.'

A shout came rolling across the waste.

'Take no notice,' ordered Biggles.

There were more shouts, and the two men started to run towards the camel lines.

'I'm afraid that's torn it,' remarked Biggles, quietly. 'Those blighters have guessed we're making off with their animals, and they've either gone to fetch help, or get mounted to pursue us. We'd better push along if I can get my brute into top gear.'

Biggles' camel, with heartrending groans, broke into a trot, and the next instant Ginger thought his end had come; but he clung to the saddle, and when the creature had settled in its stride it was not so bad. He saw that they were covering the ground at surprising speed.

For some time nothing was said. Ginger was in no state to talk. He was still wondering how long he would be able to stand the strain. Then came a shout behind. He dare not risk turning to look, but Biggles did, and announced that they were being pursued by the Toureg.

'I'm afraid they'll catch us if we don't go faster than this,' he said. 'They're as much at home on a camel as we are in a Spitfire. They know how to get most out of their beasts.'

So far Biggles had followed the gully through which they had travelled to the oasis, but they now reached a point where it fanned out to open sand for a considerable distance. Beyond was more rock. Soon after they were in the open a shot rang out, and a bullet kicked up a splash of sand in front of them. More shots followed.

Biggles looked behind him. 'They're overtaking us— quite a bunch of them,' he announced. 'Let's try to reach those rocks ahead. Hang on, I'm going to gallop. We may as well break our necks as be caught by those sheikhs behind us.'

Biggles' camel groaned again, and then broke into a

full run. Ginger gasped as his beast followed. Then he could have laughed with relief. There was no more jolting. It was like skimming through the air in a glider.

'How far away are the rocks?' he shouted.

'Two or three miles.'

Ginger risked a glance over his shoulder and saw the Arabs coming at a full gallop, flogging their beasts and uttering piercing shouts. There was also sporadic shooting. He did not know what Biggles intended doing if they reached the rocks first, but he imagined that they would stop and fight it out. He could think of nothing else. It was certain that if they kept on the Toureg would overtake them, probably shoot them down from behind at close range. For the moment it was a race for the rocks.

They reached the outcrop a bare hundred yards ahead of their pursuers, and as a camel's legs are not constructed for travelling over rock Biggles made for an opening, just such a gully as the one in which Ginger had once landed his Spitfire. A minute or two later, after they had travelled about a hundred yards in the gully, Ginger's camel, for no reason that he could see, flung up its head and swerved. Unprepared for such a manœuvre Ginger lost his balance. He made a wild grab at the animal's neck, missed it, and shot out of the saddle. The halter, to which he clung, broke his fall; then it slipped through his hands and he rolled over and over across the sand. He finished in a sitting position to see Biggles still racing on, evidently unaware of his fall.

'Hi! Biggles!' he yelled desperately.

Apparently Biggles did not hear, for he ignored the cry.

A thunder of hooves at the entrance to the gully

brought Ginger to his feet in a hurry, revolver in hand. An instant later the Arabs came pouring through the gap in the rock. They must have seen the loose camel which, having got rid of its rider, was standing on the open sand in the supercilious attitude that only these animals can adopt; possibly they saw Ginger as well, for with harsh shouts they pulled their beasts to a skidding standstill.

Ginger, without turning, backed towards the wall, revolver at the ready. He had given up all thought of escape, but was determined to do as much damage as possible before he was shot, as he knew he must be at the end of so one-sided an affair. Out of the corner of his eye he saw Biggles stop and then come tearing back. He was sorry about this, for he could not see what useful purpose Biggles hoped to serve. It looked as though he was throwing his life away uselessly.

By this time Ginger had reached the rock wall that bounded the gully, and with his back to it, in deep shadow, he brought a sharp fire to bear on the Arabs, moving his position between each shot. This was necessary, for the Arabs were shooting now—the ragged fire of undisciplined men. They appeared to have no concerted plan of attack, but with a good deal of unnecessary noise, scattered, and began to advance, each in his own way.

By this time Biggles had dismounted and was running towards the spot, keeping close against the rock. He disappeared into deep shadow, but his voice reached Ginger clearly.

'Can you get up the rock behind you from where you are?'

'No!' shouted Ginger. 'It's sheer.'

'Then retire towards me,' called Biggles. 'There's a

place here. If we can get on the rocks their camels won't be able to follow. Keep coming—I'll cover you.' Biggles' gun spat.

Ginger began to run along the gully to the point where he judged Biggles to be; but evidently the move was seen by the Arabs who, with renewed yells and more firing, began to close in. In his heart he felt that the position was hopeless, and his reaction was a sort of reckless abandon that completely eliminated anything in the nature of fear.

'Come on Biggles!' he yelled. 'Let's paste the devils!' Crouching, he turned towards the Arabs who were now fast closing in; but a moment later, to his surprise, for he could see no reason to account for it, they began to retire. Thinking perhaps the Arabs were reluctant to face his fire, with a shout of triumph he dashed forward, shooting until a click told him that his gun was empty. By this time the Arabs were in full flight; they remounted their camels and raced for the open sand. And while he was still marvelling at this extraordinary behaviour there came a sound that brought him round with a gasp. It was the hum of a powerful car. Then a headlight blazed down the gully, flooding the scene with radiance. A machine-gun began its vicious staccato chatter, and he flung himself flat as a hail of lead ripped up the sand and spattered against the rock.

For a minute or two Ginger lay where he had thrown himself, his brain in a whirl at this unexpected development. Then, as he saw the *Luftwaffe* car come tearing down the gully, and he realized what had happened, he laughed hysterically. The car dashed up, and even before it had stopped a figure with a white bandage round its head jumped out. He recognized Tex.

'Say, Ginger, what goes on?' Tex demanded.

Ginger put his gun in his pocket and leaned against the car as Taffy, Henry and Ferocity scrambled out.

Biggles strode up. 'Where the deuce have you come from?' he inquired. 'How did you get here, Tex? I thought you were on the sick list?'

'So I was, but I got well,' answered Tex, casually. 'Say, chief, what's wrong with your head?' he added, noticing Biggles' bandage.

'It got in the way of a bullet,' answered Biggles, briefly. He turned to Taffy. 'So you got the car out? Bit of luck for us; you timed your arrival very nicely.'

'Luck?' questioned Taffy. 'Why, we were looking for you!'

Biggles frowned. 'Don't be ridiculous. How could you have known we were in the desert?'

'Well, it was this way, look you,' returned Taffy. 'When we got the car out we took it back to Salima to refuel, and then came out on patrol as you suggested. We heard the two Spits go home, and soon afterwards, while we were still cruising towards Wadi Umbo, what we took to be the Rapide. So we—thinking everything was all right—had a cigarette, and were just thinking of going home when we got a radio signal from Algy, who was back in the Defiant at Salima. He said the Rapide had landed, but you and Ginger weren't on board. He reckoned you must have been left at Wadi Umbo, but if you hadn't been captured you wouldn't stay there. He thought you might start to walk back, so he asked us to come and meet you. Then we heard the shooting, and here we are. That's all there was to it.'

Biggles smiled. 'Nice piece of staff work, Taffy. Matter of fact we were trying to get home on a couple of camels, but Ginger stalled and made a crash landing.

181

The Toureg were on our trail, and for a minute or two things looked a bit gloomy. As I said just now, you couldn't have timed your arrival better. But we mustn't stand talking here. I've things to do. The sky will be stiff with Messerschmitts presently. What's the time?'

'Half-past three.'

Biggles whistled. 'Late as that? Then we certainly have no time to lose. Von Zoyton has imported several loads of paratroops, and they'll be calling on us presently. As we're fixed if they once get their feet on the ground in Salima they'll make a shambles of the place. Stand fast. I'm going to send a signal to Algy.'

'Don't forget von Zoyton will hear you,' put in Ferocity.

'Oh, no, he won't,' replied Biggles. 'All that's left of his radio equipment, I hope, is a heap of cinders.' He went into the car and sat down at the instrument, and was soon in touch with Salima. Having assured Algy that he and Ginger were safe, he ordered the Rapide to proceed immediately to Karga, taking the released prisoners, together with Algy, Angus, Bertie and Tug, who were to return forthwith in the four Spitfires. He closed by saying that the car was on its way home and should be back before dawn.

'If that works out without any snags, by dawn we should have six Spits and the Defiant,' announced Biggles to the others, who were watching him. 'Von Zoyton will suppose that we are down to two Spitfires—not enough to stop his Messerschmitts and Junkers. He'll strike, as he thinks, before we can get help. I should say his entire crowd will be over at dawn, or soon after. We've got to get those troop carriers before they can unload or Salima will be wiped out. To-morrow ought to see the showdown. Let's get home.'

Chapter 16
The Battle of Salima

After a tiring journey, during which Biggles often dozed, the car arrived back at the oasis just before six o'clock. The moon had set, and the darkness that precedes the dawn had closed over the wilderness. Flight-Sergeant Smyth met the car to announce that coffee and biscuits were waiting in the mess tent. He was in charge at the oasis, all the officers having gone to Karga in the Rapide to fetch the Spitfires. Biggles, pale and red-eyed, led the way to the tent and gulped down the welcome refreshment.

'Now listen, everybody,' he said. 'That includes you, flight-sergeant. I can give you all ten minutes for a bath and brush up; then we must get busy. Von Zoyton has been reinforced by four Junkers troop carriers. He has about sixty paratroops, to say nothing of the men of his own unit. He aims to wipe us out completely. He can want air-borne troops for no other purpose. We know now how the Nazis do this operation. The Junkers will either crash-land, or unload in the air under a protecting screen of Messerschmitts. We may safely assume that von Zoyton will lead the show in person. If we had more machines I shouldn't wait for him to come. I should have a crack at Wadi Umbo before he could get started. But we can't do that with only three machines, leaving Salima unprotected. The Karga Spitfires may be here in time to give us a hand, or they may not. I hope they will. It will be a close thing,

183

anyway. I reckon the earliest the four Spitfires can get here will be about seven o'clock—twenty minutes after sun-up. Von Zoyton is bound to attack before the heat of the day. If he comes at the crack of dawn we shall have to carry the whole weight of the attack with what we've got. Every minute he delays after that gives us a better chance. But the point is this. If those para-troops get on the ground in this oasis, we're sunk. They carry grenades, flame-throwers, sub-machine guns—in fact, everything needed for their job. Not only have we none of these things here, bar a couple of Tommy guns, but we are outnumbered six to one. Obviously, then, we must at all costs prevent the Junkers from getting through. Presently I shall go with the flight-sergeant and fix up such ground defences as we can manage. The two Spitfires and the Defiant will leave the ground before dawn and go to meet the enemy.'

'Do you think you are fit to fly?' asked Ginger anxiously.

'I shall fly one of the Spitfires,' answered Biggles coldly. 'You will fly the other, because you know better than anyone else how I work in a case like this. Taffy, you will fly the Defiant. Sorry, Tex, but you and Henry will have to take charge of things on the ground. Don't look so glum; if those Nazis get their feet on the floor you'll have plenty to do, believe me. The three aircraft will leave the ground in fifteen minutes. That's all. Now go and get cleaned up. Ginger, Taffy, Ferocity, stand fast.'

After the others had filed out, Biggles turned to those who were to fly. 'This looks like being a tough show,' he said. 'I shall, of course, try to spring a surprise, for which reason I shall take you up to the ceiling. The Messerschmitts are bound to fly above the Junkers. I aim to go right down through them, which should upset them, if only for a few seconds. In a show like this seconds count. I shall go after the Junkers. The others will do what they can to keep the Messerschmitts off my tail. In your case, Taffy, I think your best plan would be to adopt the tactics Ball* brought to a fine art in the last war. He used to throw himself straight into the middle of the enemy formation and then skid all over the sky, browning** the whole bunch, and generally acting as though his idea was to ram anyone who got in his way. If you can get the enemy split up they'll have to watch each other to prevent collisions. Make the most of that. Ginger, do what you can to keep my tail clear while I deal with the Junkers. I'll meet you at the machines in ten minutes.'

Biggles had a new dressing put on his head, and a quick wash, which freshened him up considerably. When he went out he found the oasis a hive of activity. Arms were being distributed and men posted at strategical points. Airmen were struggling under loads of ammunition. Biggles made a quick round of the defences, and then joined Ginger, Taffy and Ferocity at the machines. For a little while, smoking a cigarette, he gazed at the eastern horizon; but as soon as the first pale flush of dawn appeared he trod his cigarette into the ground.

'Come on,' he said. 'It's going to be heavy going while it lasts, but it shouldn't last long. To-day will see the end of either Salima or Wadi Umbo. When we

---

* Albert Ball, British World War One fighter pilot who shot down 44 planes. He was killed in 1917.
** Slang: shooting his machine-gun at as many aircraft as possible.

sight the enemy stay close to me until I give the signal to peel off.'

Biggles swung himself into his cockpit and started the engine; he sat still for a few seconds with his engine idling, and then roared into air which, at that hour, was as soft as milk. Swinging round slowly towards the northwest he settled down to climb.

The radiance behind him became a living flame, and when some minutes later the rim of the sun showed above the horizon to put out the last lingering stars he smiled faintly with satisfaction. It was dawn. According to his calculations, Algy and the Karga Spitfires were still a hundred miles away, but every passing minute knocked five miles off the intervening distance. A glance at his altimeter showed that he was now at twenty thousand feet, but he continued to climb until Salima was no more than a lonely islet in an ocean of sand that rolled away to infinity. Ahead, the sky was clear. Biggles examined it methodically, above and below, section by section, for the tiny black specks that would be his first view of the enemy; but they were not in sight. At twenty-two thousand he turned on the oxygen and went on up to twenty-five thousand, at the same time turning a few miles to the north of a straight line between the two oases. Not for a moment did he relax in his ceaseless scrutiny of the sky. His face was like a mask, expressionless. Only his eyes seemed alive.

At last he saw what he was looking for. He spotted the four Junkers first; they were flying a good deal lower than he expected, not higher, he judged, than six thousand feet. Five thousand feet above them, and about a mile behind, four Messerschmitt 109's followed the same course, like sharks in the wake of a convoy. Where were the rest? Lifting his eyes Biggles saw three more machines, perhaps five thousand feet above and a mile behind, the middle layer. All were on a straight course for Salima. Biggles had anticipated this, which was why he had edged to the north. He was anxious to avoid being seen before he struck. The Nazis had adopted a typical battle formation; there was nothing about it to make him change his plans.

As the top layer drew near he frowned. There was something odd about them. Then he saw what it was. They were not all the same type. The leading machine was a Messerschmitt 109 F., an improvement on the 109. This settled one question. If von Zoyton was in the party he would be in the new machine. Where the aircraft had come from Biggles did not know, nor did he care. The machine was there, and that was all that mattered. With the Nazi ace at the joystick it was far and away the most formidable member of the hostile force, worth, probably half a dozen ordinary Messerschmitt 109's flown by pilots of average ability.

The enemy machines were still flying straight towards Salima. Biggles allowed them to pass. He felt sure that not one of the Nazis had seen the three British machines sitting nine thousand feet above them, or some move would have been made, some signal given. Von Zoyton would have placed himself between them and his vulnerable troop carriers. Once behind them, Biggles knew that there would be still less chance of discovery, for von Zoyton and his pack, if expecting trouble, would look for it ahead, in the direction of Salima; so Biggles swung round in a wide half-circle that brought him about two miles behind the enemy machines, on the same course, and still well above. He moistened his lips and braced his body. The time had come. He turned his head to look at Ginger and Taffy in turn. They were both watching him. He nodded. Then, with his lips set in a straight line by the strain of the impending action he thrust the control column forward. With a wail of protest the nose of the Spitfire tilted down until it was in line with the top layer of enemy machines. Speed, now, was what he needed, if he was to reach his real objective—the four Junkers troop carriers, which from his height looked like four bloated locusts crawling across the dunes.

Forward and still farther forward Biggles thrust the joystick, the needle of the speed indicator keeping a quivering record of his rate of dive. The top layer of Messerschmitts seemed to float up towards him as the distance closed between them. At any moment now von Zoyton might glance in his reflector and see what was coming down behind him, but so far he had not moved. The 109 F. was still cruising on even keel. Biggles could see every detail of the machine clearly. He studied it dispassionately, noting that von Zoyton had even found time to paint his nose and rudder blue; but his hand made no move towards the firing button. For the moment he was not concerned with Messerschmitts; his target was the machines that alone could wipe out Salima beyond recovery. His Spitfire, nearly vertical, flashed past the noses of the three Messerschmitts.

He went straight on down towards the second formation. He knew that von Zoyton would be tearing after him now, but confident that the Nazi could not overtake him before he reached the Junkers he did not trouble to look back. If all the three Messerschmitts were on his tail, as he guessed they would be, they would have to be careful to avoid collision with the second layer when he went through it. In this way he was for the moment making their superior numbers a handicap, not an asset.

He flashed past the middle layer of the four 109's like a streak of lightning and the Junkers lay clear below, as helpless as whales basking on a calm sea. Down—down—down he tore, his airscrew howling like a lost soul in agony. A glance in the reflector now revealed a sight that brought a mirthless smile to his lips. The sky behind seemed full of machines, some near, some far, but all following the line of his meteoric drive. Satisfied that he had achieved his object in throwing the Messerschmitts into a confusion from which they would take a minute to recover, he took the nearest Junkers in his sights. But he held his fire. The range was still too long, and he had no ammunition to waste on chancy shooting.

Not until he was within five hundred feet did his hand move to the firing button. Then his guns flamed, and the Spitfire vibrated under the weight of metal it discharged. His face did not change expression as he saw his tracers cutting white lines through the air into the fat body of the troop carrier. A fraction less pressure on the control column and the hail of bullets crept along the fuselage to the cockpit. Splinters flew before their shattering impact. A tiny spark of fire appeared, glowing ever brighter.

Biggles waited for no more. A touch on the rudder-bar brought his nose in line with the leading Junkers. Again his guns spat death. Again splinters flew as his bullets ripped through the swastika-decorated machine, which staggered drunkenly before making a swerving turn, nose down.

So close was Biggles by this time that he had to pull up sharply to avoid collision. While in the zoom, the grunt of guns behind him made him kick out his left foot, which brought him skidding round as though struck by a whirlwind. He had a fleeting view of a 109 as it flashed past. He jerked up his nose, fired a quick burst at it, and then snatched a glance around to see what was happening.

The picture presented was one that only a fighter pilot sees. The sky was full of aircraft, banking, diving and zooming, as much to avoid collision as to take aim. From the eddying core of the dogfight a number of machines appeared to have been flung out. A Messerschmitt was going down in flames. Another Messerschmitt and the Defiant, locked in a ghastly embrace, were flat-spinning earthward. There was no one in the cockpit of the Defiant. From the Messerschmitt the pilot was just scrambling out. Flung aft by the slipstream he hurtled against the tail unit and bounced off into space. A Spitfire and the blue-nosed 109 F were waltzing round each other. Von Zoyton seemed to be trying to break away, but every time he straightened out the Spitfire dashed in, guns blazing, forcing him to turn. Below, only two Junkers were in sight. They were some distance apart. One was making for the oasis, nose down; the other was circling as if the pilot could not make up his mind what to do. All this Biggles saw in an instant of time. Without hesitation he roared down after the Junkers that was still heading for Salima.

Again he held his fire until the last moment, and then poured in a long, deadly burst. The bullets missed the fuselage at which he aimed; they struck the port wing near the root, and the effect was as if the wing had encountered a bandsaw. It began to bend upwards. The slight play at the tip, always perceptible in a big metal wing, became a regular flap, horrible to watch. Then the sheet metal began to tear like paper; the wing broke clean off, and whirling aft, passed so close to Biggles before he could turn that he flinched, thinking that it must strike him. The Junkers rolled on its side, while from the cabin, in quick succession, the paratroops dived into space.

Biggles turned away, and looking for the last surviving troop carrier saw that it had gone on, and had nearly reached Salima. Below and behind it parachutes were hanging in the air like scraps of paper windblown. It had succeeded, or almost succeeded, in its allotted task, and there was nothing he could do about it—except hope that those at the oasis would be able to deal with any paratroops that managed to reach it. His anxiety on this score was shortlived, and he smiled when he saw the armoured car burst from the trees and race towards the place where the paratroops would land.

Satisfied, he turned away. His head was now aching unmercifully, and he was almost overcome by a fit of nausea. He knew that he had been flying on his nerves; that he had already overtaxed his physical strength and was not in a condition to carry on the fight; yet he could not bring himself to leave the air to a victorious enemy. Worried by a growing sense of unreality he began to fear that he might faint. There seemed to be very few machines about, and these were widely scattered; but he could still see four Messerschmitts. One was retiring, but the other three were converging on him. Where was Ginger? Glancing down he was just in time to see the Spitfire strike the ground flat on the bottom of its fuselage, bounce high, stall, and then bury its nose in the yielding sand. Ginger was out of the fight.

Dry-lipped, feeling sick and faint, Biggles turned to meet the Messerschmitts. The matter would soon be over one way or another. He knew he could not hang out for more than a few minutes. The Messerschmitts seemed to be a long way away. He could not think what they were doing. He found it hard to think at all. From their behaviour it seemed that the hostile aircraft were hesitating, inclined to break off the combat. Setting his teeth he flew straight at them. Then a movement to the right caught his eye, and he saw four machines in a scattered line roaring towards the scene. For a moment he stared at them uncomprehendingly. Then he understood why the Messerschmitts were packing up. The Karga Spitfires had arrived.

But what were they doing? They appeared to dance in the air like midges over a garden path on a summer night. They became blurred, like a photograph out of focus. The sky was beginning to turn black. Biggles bit his lip until it hurt. His hands were trembling, clammy; cold sweat broke out on his face. 'My God!' he thought. 'I'm going to faint.' Pulling back the cockpit cover he tried to rise, to throw himself out, but all the strength seemed to have left his body. Abandoning the joystick, he used both hands to raise himself, but as the full blast of the slipstream struck him he paused, gulping in the refreshing air. It revived him. He began to feel better. Things began to clear, so he slid back into his seat, cut the engine, and began a steady glide down. At first he was content to lose height, but as his strength returned he looked around and set a course for the oasis.

His landing was purely automatic, although he

would have run on into the trees had not a mechanic had the wit to dash out and grab a wing tip so that the machine slewed round, raking up the sand. Biggles switched off and sat still, limp from reaction. Flight-Sergeant Smyth's face, pale with concern, appeared beside him.

'Are you all right, sir?'

'Yes, I'm all right,' answered Biggles weakly. 'Drink—get me a drink.'

The flight sergeant shouted and a man came running.

Biggles drank from the water bottle, carelessly, the water gushing unheeded down his chin and over the front of his jacket. 'Phew!' he gasped. 'That's better. Give me a hand down, flight sergeant. I'm a bit shaky on my pins. What's happened?'

'Nothing much, sir. We soon mopped up the umbrella men*.'

Tex appeared. With the flight sergeant he got Biggles down and steered him towards the palms.

'I'm all right now,' declared Biggles. 'Let me sit in the shade for a minute. I must have got a touch of sun.'

'What you've got,' said Tex deliberately, 'is a touch of overwork.'

Biggles sat down and had another drink. 'What about Ginger?'

'He's all right,' answered Tex. 'He ran out of slugs and came down for more—but he was in too much of a hurry considering his undercart was shot to bits and wouldn't *unstick***. He came a lovely belly-flopper.

* R.A.F. slang for paratroops
** i e. his wheels wouldn't descend into landing position.

193

He's got a black eye and a split lip. The last I saw of him he was sousing his face in a bucket of water.'

'What about Taffy and Ferocity?'

'This looks like 'em, coming now.'

Looking up, Biggles saw them walking towards the oasis, dragging their brollies. Taffy was limping. They seemed to be having a heated altercation.

'Look at them, the fools,' muttered Biggles, beginning to laugh. 'Tex, go and stop them, or they'll be fighting each other in a minute.'

Presently they came up. Taffy was incoherent. 'He did it, look you!' he shouted.

'Did what?' demanded Biggles.

'Broke my Defiant. I wanted to go one way, whatsoever—'

'And he wanted to go another way?' put in Biggles.

'Yes,' agreed Taffy disgustedly.

'And between you you ran into a Messerschmitt? You see what happens when two people try to fly the same kite?' said Biggles sadly. 'Where are the Karga Spitfires?'

'Chasing the Huns back home,' grunted Taffy.

Biggles started. 'Hello! What the dickens . . . what's this coming?'

They all looked up as a deep-throated roar announced the approach of a heavy aircraft.

'It's a civil machine,' said Tex. 'It must be the freighter—bound for the West Coast. Sure, that's it.'

'Do you know,' said Biggles, 'I'd clean forgotten all about it. No matter, it ought to be able to get through without any trouble. If it doesn't—well, I can't help it. I've never been so tired in my life. When Algy comes back tell him to carry on.'

Biggles lay back, closed his eyes, and was instantly asleep.

195

Chapter 17

The Last Round

The sun was fast falling towards the western horizon when Biggles awoke. He was still lying under the palms, although someone had put a pillow under his head. Ginger, his face black and blue, lay stretched out beside him. The flight sergeant was standing by. Everything was strangely quiet. Biggles took one look at the sun and then called the N.C.O.

'Flight sergeant, what do you mean by letting me sleep so long?' he demanded.

'Mr. Lacey's orders, sir. He said you were to sleep on.'

'Where is he?'

'Resting, sir.'

'All right. Tell all the officers I want to see them in the mess tent right away.'

'Very good, sir.'

Biggles prodded Ginger. 'Here, snap out of it.'

Ginger started and sat up. 'What, again?' he moaned.

'We've only just started,' asserted Biggles. 'Come on over to the tent.'

'How are you feeling?'

'Fine—well enough to clean up Wadi Umbo. When that's done you can sleep for a week if you like.'

Biggles walked over to the mess tent, where he found the officers assembling. Addressing them he said,

'What's the idea, everyone going to sleep in the middle of a job?'

'But I say, old centurion, I thought we'd finished,' protested Bertie, adjusting his monocle.

'You mean—you got von Zoyton?'

'Well—er—no. 'Fraid we didn't quite do that.'

'What happened to him?'

'He gathered his warriors around him and departed for a less strenuous locality—if you see what I mean.'

Biggles turned to Algy. 'Let's have the facts. What happened after I came down? The last thing I remember—I must admit I couldn't see very clearly—was the four Karga Spitfires about to pass the time of day with what remained of the Messerschmitts.'

'They just pushed off home,' announced Algy. 'We followed them some way, and then, as I didn't know what had happened here, I thought we'd better come back.'

'So they got away?'

'Yes.'

Biggles turned to Flight-Sergeant Smyth, who was standing by. 'What's the state of our aircraft?'

'Five Spitfires, sir, including your own, which has been damaged by gunshots, although it's still serviceable.'

Biggles nodded. 'That should be enough.'

'Enough for what?' asked Algy.

'Enough for a show-down.'

'What's the hurry?'

'None, except that this squadron doesn't leave a job half done. Anyway, I don't feel like sitting here panting in this heat while von Zoyton sends for replacements and remusters his forces. Never leave your enemy while he's feeling sore; either depart or finish him off, or he'll come back and get you. That's what my first C.O. taught me, and I've always found it to be good policy. We can't leave here without orders, so we must go to Wadi Umbo, drive von Zoyton out, and make the place uninhabitable for some time to come. Not until we've done that can we report the route safe.'

'How can we destroy an oasis?'

'By putting the water hole out of commission.'

'When are you going?'

'Now. I'm going to wipe out the rest of von Zoyton's machines, either on the ground or in the air—he can have it which way he likes. You'd better toss up to see who's going to fly the other four machines. Don't fight over it. It won't be a picnic. Von Zoyton has just imported a nice line in pom-poms. Someone will have to stay in charge here, but the rest, those who are not flying, can make a sortie in the direction of Wadi Umbo in the car. We'd better get a move on, or it will be dark.'

Ten minutes later the five Spitfires took off in vee formation and headed north-west. Behind Biggles were Algy, Bertie, Henry Harcourt and Ginger. Angus remained in charge at Salima; the others were following in the car.

This time Biggles did not climb for height. The five machines, rocking in the intense heat flung up by the tortured earth, annihilated space as they raced low over rock and sand and stunted camel thorn. With his head newly bandaged, Biggles did not beat about the arid atmosphere; he went as straight as an arrow for Wadi Umbo, and inside half an hour, just as the sun was falling like a golden ball beyond its ragged fringe of palms, he was striking at the oasis with everything his guns had in them.

When the Spitfires arrived Biggles caught the flash of an airscrew in the clearing that was used by the enemy as an aircraft park. Whether the machine had just come in, or was just going off on a mission, he did not know. He never knew. He gave it a long burst as he dived, and watched his tracer shells curving languidly towards the stationary aircraft. Skimming over the tree-tops he saw something else, something that filled him with savage glee. There was quite a number of men about. Most of them were dashing for their battle stations, but he did not trouble about them. In a small bay of the clearing he saw a Messerschmitt 109. Men were working on it, hauling in a serpentine pipe-line which seemed to connect it with the ground. The machine was being refuelled with a hand pump. This told him something he did not know before—the position of the fuel dump.

Zooming, and banking steeply, he saw that the first dive of the five Spitfires had not been without effect. Two of the Messerschmitts were burning fiercely; another was so close that it was in imminent danger of catching fire. Men were dragging it away, but a burst from Biggles' guns sent them running pell-mell for cover.

He now concentrated on the fuel dump to the exclusion of all else. Three bursts he fired as he tore down, and at the end of the third he saw what he hoped to see—a burst of flame spurting from the ground. Then he had to pull out to avoid hitting the trees.

Surveying the scene as he banked he saw that what was happening was what he had feared might happen at Salima. Under the hammering of five converging Spitfires the oasis was already half hidden behind a curtain of smoke through which leapt orange flames.

199

A vast cloud of oily black smoke rising sluggishly into the air from the clearing told him that the oil was alight. The hut that had housed the prisoners, roofed as it was of tinder-dry palm fronds, was a roaring bonfire from which erupted pieces of blazing thatch that set fire to what they fell upon—the dry grass, tents and stores.

The pom-pom gunners had no chance. Streams of shells soared upwards, but the flak* came nowhere near the aircraft, and Biggles knew that the gunners were simply shooting blindly through the pall of smoke. Men appeared, running out of the inferno, some beating their jackets, which were alight, on the ground.

With the whole oasis hidden under the rolling smoke there was nothing more Biggles could do. Like the others, who had stopped shooting for the same reason, he started circling. And presently, as he watched, he saw a lorry emerge from the smoke and head north. He could just see it through the murk. Presently another lorry, followed by a car, emerged, and he knew that the oasis was being evacuated.

From the beginning of the affair he had not seen the 109 F., so he could only assume that it had been burnt, and that von Zoyton was moving off in one of the surface vehicles. There was nothing more to be done, so, well satisfied with the result of the raid, he cruised a little to the north to count the departing vehicles before returning to Salima. As he flew towards the drifting smoke which by this time had been carried high by the heat-created up-currents, he thought he saw a grey shadow flit across a thin patch. He watched the spot closely, but not seeing anything concluded that

* Exploding anti-aircraft shells.

he had been mistaken, and went on through the smoke to get in a position from which he would be able to count the surface craft. Presently he saw them. Five vehicles and a line of camels were racing towards the north. He watched them for a moment or two, tempted to shoot them up; and it is an odd fact that had he done so, as he realized an instant later, he would have regretted using what little ammunition remained in his guns. As it was, giving way to a quixotic and perhaps misplaced chivalry, he refrained from making the plight of the desert-bound refugees more perilous than it was. So he turned away, leisurely, and was still turning when a movement in his reflector caused him to move so fast that it seemed impossible that he could have found time to think. Kicking out his foot and flinging the joystick over on the same side, he spun round in a wild bank while a stream of tracer flashed past his wing tip. His mouth went dry at the narrowness of his escape. A split-second later and the bullets, fired from close range, must have riddled his machine. A Messerschmitt 109 F., travelling at tremendous speed, howled past in the wake of its bullets, and Biggles' lips curled in a sneer of self-contempt for so nearly allowing himself to be caught napping.

That von Zoyton was in the Messerschmitt he knew from the way it was being handled. The shadow in the smoke was now explained. The Nazi had been stalking him for some minutes. There was nothing wrong with that. It was all in the game, for in air combat there are no rules. All is fair. There is no question of hitting below the belt. There are no rounds. The formula is simple—get your man. How, when and where, doesn't matter as long as you get him.

The Messerschmitt was turning on the top of its

zoom, obviously with the idea of renewing the attack, and Biggles smiled at the thought of how annoyed the Nazi would be at having lost the supreme advantage of surprise. The other Spitfires were out of sight behind the ever-rising cloud of smoke. Biggles was glad they were. He hoped they would remain there. It would simplify matters. He would not have to identify a machine before shooting at it and the question of collision could not arise, as it might if too many machines became involved. He and von Zoyton had the field to themselves; that suited him, and it would no doubt suit the Nazi.

The two machines were now both at the same height. Both were banking, each striving to get behind the other. Biggles, remembering the stunt which, according to rumour, had helped von Zoyton to pile up his big score, watched his opponent with a sense of alert curiosity. His hand tightened on the control column. He knew that he had a redoubtable opponent, and that could only mean a battle to the death, a battle in which one false move would have fatal results. Neither he nor the Nazi had ever been beaten; now one of them must taste defeat. Within a few minutes either the Spitfire or the Messerschmitt would lie, a crumpled wreck, upon the desert sand.

Both aircraft had now tightened the turn until they were in vertical bank, one on each side of a circle perhaps three hundred feet across. Both were flying on full throttle. Biggles' joystick was right back; so, he knew, was von Zoyton's. Neither could turn much faster. The circle might tighten a little, that was all. After that the end would probably depend upon sheer speed combined with manoeuvrability. The machine that could overtake the other would get in the first burst. If von Zoyton was going to pull his trick, it would come, must come, within the next few seconds.

Round and round tore the two machines as though braced on an invisible pivot. Tighter and tighter became the circle as each pilot tried to get the other in his sights. Engines roared, their slipstreams howling over the sleek fuselages. Biggles' face and lips were bloodless, for the strain was tremendous. He lost count of space, and time, and of the perpendicular. His eyes never left his opponent. It was no use shooting, for the blue tail was always just a little in front of his sights, in the same way that his own tail was just in front of von Zoyton's sights. He knew that the Nazi was undergoing just the same strain, as he, too, strove to pull in that little extra that would bring the Spitfire before his guns. Biggles could see his opponent clearly. He could feel his eyes on him.

He was beginning to wonder if the story of the trick was, after all, only a rumour, when it happened. He was ready. He had been ready all the time. But even then he could not understand how the Messerschmitt managed to cut across the diameter of the circle. All he knew was that the blue airscrew boss was pointing at him, guns streaming flame. He could hear the bullets ripping through his fuselage. At that moment he thought—no, he was convinced—that the Nazi had him cold, and his reaction was one not uncommon with air fighters. If he was going to crash he would take his opponent with him. Turning at a speed that would have torn the wings off a less robust aircraft, he whirled round in a second turn so flat that centrifugal force clamped him in his seat. But he was straight in the track of his enemy, facing him head-on. His thumb came down viciously on the firing button.

For a fleeting instant the air was filled with tracer as the two machines, travelling at top speed, faced each other across a distance of under two hundred feet. It seemed that nothing could prevent collision. Both pilots fired simultaneously as they came in line. In that tremendous moment Biggles could see his shells and bullets streaming like living sparks into the blue nose, and ripping splinters off the slim fuselage. He was suffering the same punishment. Pieces of metal were leaping from his engine cowling. Splinters flew. Instruments burst, spurting glass. His compass seemed to explode, flinging liquid in his face. Some went into his eyes, and he gasped at the pain. He flew on blindly, trying desperately to see. He felt, rather than heard, the roar of von Zoyton's machine, and braced himself for the shock of collision. It did not come.

When he was able to see again he found himself spinning, dangerously near the ground. Pulling out, he had to swerve wildly to miss a parachute that was falling across his nose. Below, the Messerschmitt, with broken wings, lay crumpled on the sand.

By the time he had turned von Zoyton was on the ground, shaking off his harness. This done, he looked up and raised his right arm in the Nazi salute. Biggles, a curious smile on his pale face, flew past him very low, and banking so that he could be seen, lifted his hand in a parting signal. He could see the German cars, a quarter of a mile away, heading for the spot, so, satisfied that the vanquished pilot would not be left to die of thirst, he climbed up through the smoke to find the four Spitfires still circling, evidently waiting. They converged on him at once and took up formation, while Biggles, feeling suddenly weary, set a course for Salima.

When, in the swiftly fading desert twilight, he got back to the base, he was not a little surprised to see a Lysander standing in the lengthening shadows of the palms on the edge of the landing ground. After landing he taxied over to it, and jumped down to meet a drill-clad figure wearing the badges of rank of a Group Captain. He recognized one of the senior Operations officers of R.A.F. Headquarters, Middle East.

Biggles saluted. 'Good evening, sir.'

The Group Captain returned the salute. ''Evening, Bigglesworth. I've just run down to see how you're getting on. The Air Vice-Marshal is getting a bit worried about his route. He has just learned that von Zoyton and his *staffel* are somewhere in this region.'

'We discovered that too, sir,' answered Biggles, smiling. 'But I think we can use the past tense. The last time I saw von Zoyton, less than an hour ago, he was standing on a sand dune near Oasis Wadi Umbo looking fed up to the teeth.'

The Group Captain stared. 'You mean—you've actually seen him?'

Biggles grinned. 'You bet we have. And he's seen us—hasn't he, chaps?' Biggles glanced round the circle of officers, all of whom had now returned to the oasis.

Understanding began to dawn in the Group Captain's expression. His eyes twinkled. 'What was von Zoyton fed up about?' he inquired.

Biggles lit a cigarette. 'Well, in the first place, we had just had a spot of argument, and he got the worst of it. On top of that my boys had made a bonny bonfire of his base. I don't think he'll be using it again for some time; in fact, I don't think anybody will. The survivors have pulled out in what remained of their surface craft, heading north. You can tell the Air Vice-

Marshall that as far as hostile aircraft are concerned his blistering route is okay.'

'Good work!'

'It was hot work—in more senses than one,' returned Biggles, dryly.

'And you left von Zoyton standing in the desert?'

'I did, sir.'

'You might have had a shot at him.'

Biggles made a gesture of annoyance. 'So I might! Do you know, sir, I clean forgot.'

The Group Captain laughed. 'Same old spirit. Well, there's something to be said for it. You're a funny fellow, Biggles.'

'Maybe you're right, sir,' returned Biggles. 'But if you don't mind me saying so, this hell's kitchen is fast ruining my sense of humour. Now the job's done, perhaps the Air Vice-Marshal will find us a station where the grass grows green and the fruit doesn't come out of cans.'

'I'm sure he will,' declared the Group Captain.

'In that case, sir, you won't mind if we throw a little celebration? If you're not in a hurry to get back, how about being our guest?'

The Group Captain looked round the ring of weary, grimy, sun-tanned faces.

'The honour's mine,' he said.